RHYTHMS OF
THE HEART

Published by Sapere Books.

20 Windermere Drive, Leeds, England, LS17 7UZ,
United Kingdom

saperebooks.com

ISBN: 978-1-80055-773-4

RHYTHMS OF THE HEART

The Moondreams House Romance Novels

Book One

Ros Rendle

Also in the Moondreams House series:
Lost and Found
Finding Happiness

To Janina Mossman at Nene School of Dancing for hours of skilful teaching
and to Janet and Catherine for their friendship through learning together.

CHAPTER 1

Annie puffed as she rushed along the busy pavement, dodging other people in an equal hurry.

Earlier, the morning had blundered into her increasingly disturbing dreams. She was always running, but she could never catch up with whatever it was she chased. Sometimes she was aware of a person ahead who turned and laughed, but she couldn't see a face, which made her frustration and anxiety worse. Once, she was in a series of corridors wearing a yellow dress and pushing a pram, which was never going to happen now, even though she was still of the age — just about. Usually, she was in a forest with the trees meeting far above to create a dense, shadowy alley.

When a child, Annie's dreams had been treasured, and she remembered trying to fall back into the fantasies as they seeped away. They'd been moon dreams, the best kind. Back then, as she'd awoken, there'd been the smell of toast or bacon and the muted sound of the radio percolating from downstairs. With a sigh, she'd thrown back the covers and padded down to greet Mummy and Daddy with a kiss and a bear hug.

A motorbike roared by and made Annie's heart race, jerking her back to the present. She glanced at her watch and resumed her rush to the library, avoiding shopping bags and stepping around splodges of gum on the pavement outside the dilapidated nightclub and the re-vamped College Arms, which proclaimed itself a wine bar these days. If she hurried, she might just get the book she'd ordered and still make the 12.14 bus.

These thoughts occupied her mind as she hurried through the library door and collided with someone.

Her bag fell from her shoulder as she was spun around, spilling its contents all over the floor. In confusion and irritation, she blew out her cheeks and expelled a great gust of air as she bent down to scoop up her keys, tampons, purse and phone. She was reaching for an ancient packet of mints and a lipstick when the broad and weathered hand of her assailant passed them to her. She looked up in surprise, then drew back from the waft of beer that emanated from the face before her.

Looking again, she realised she knew the man, although she hadn't seen him in a long while. "My goodness. Is it Harry? Harry Moon?"

The last time they'd met must have been more than twenty years before. He'd been thinner of face then, and clean shaven. Not that he had much of a beard now. More a shadow that was turning a tired grey, making him look scruffy. Back then her head had fitted neatly against his collarbone as they'd shared the last dance at the school disco. His arms had been warm around her shoulders, and she had been thrilled that it was she who he had chosen for this dance. Then he had been one of the tallest most handsome boys in their year, part of the 'in' crowd that all the boys and girls were happy to be around. When he asked her to dance, her heart had soared. Aware of the dagger looks from some girls who were not her especial friends, she hadn't cared. She had been so pleased to be enveloped by his arms holding her close. The comfort of his warmth and the tang of woody citrus aftershave assailing her nostrils made her insides swoop. She had been so proud to be with him. They had shared a brief meeting of the lips before the lights went up. It was hardly a kiss. She could still remember the sensation, though. She would have liked it to be longer and deeper. Perhaps he wasn't that experienced after all.

That relationship had ended before it had even begun, both shying away from comments and teasing friends. They didn't miss a dig at boys who dated girls in the same school. Although not ravishingly good-looking, Harry's blond hair and footballer's physique had made him stand out. But his intense blue eyes had always been his best feature. Those same eyes, now with crinkles at the corners, surveyed Annie apologetically.

"Excuse me," a tall, thin man said as he stepped around them both. They were kneeling and staring at each other.

Annie scrambled to her feet and swung her bag back onto her shoulder. Harry clambered upright, too, with another drift of beery breath. "Sorry. I know you…" He looked puzzled.

"It's okay. It was a long time ago, and I've changed quite a bit. I'm Annie. I was Annie Holmes." She dusted down her skirt and endeavoured to tuck her hair behind her ears, feeling shabby and unkempt. *Mind you*, she thought, *he's no picture anymore.*

"Oh, I haven't forgotten who you are. Not at all. Look, I'm so sorry about knocking into you. Fact is, I was miles away. At a bit of a loose end, I suppose." He cast his eyes down.

"I have a book to collect," Annie said, casting about for something to say and avoiding eye contact.

"Oh, sorry," Harry said again. "I better let you get on."

Annie glanced at her watch and sighed. "I shan't get my bus now, and there isn't another for an hour. Shall we go and get a drink somewhere and have a catch-up?"

"I better not have any more to drink," he said, looking penitent.

"Oh, I didn't mean alcohol. There's always the café upstairs here. Well, only if you want to."

"Sorry. Yes, I'd like to. You could get your book, and I'll go and get them in and meet you up there," Harry said. "Tea? Or would you prefer coffee?"

As they parted, Annie thought, *Get them in? Sounds like pub speak, and he certainly smelled of ale. I wonder if this is wise. People change with time, and not always for the better.*

Ten minutes later, they were seated opposite each other. It was quiet, apart from the clatter of china behind the counter and the mutter of voices from across the room.

"Well," Harry said.

"Mmm," Annie muttered. Then she made the effort that he seemed unable to summon. "What have you been doing since school?"

"Huh, this and that." He looked out of the window and she followed his gaze to the grey clouds. "Did you say you have a bus to catch? I hope it doesn't rain. Looks like you have no coat or umbrella."

He always was kind, she remembered. Annie murmured lines of the song that popped into her head again. "But it's raining, raining in my heart." *A rumba*, she thought. Her background in dance was never far from her thoughts and that song had been the rhythm of her soul for so many months.

He looked mystified, so she smiled, shook her head, as she watched him fill his teaspoon from the spout of the sugar jar and stir it into his tea. "So where are you living?"

She named one of the villages that had been subsumed by the areas of development all around the city. "It's alright. Small, modern, but easy to keep going, now I'm on my own."

"Oh?"

"I'm not Holmes now. It's Annie Ellis, but my husband died eighteen months ago." She was amazed that she could utter those words after months of trying to avoid speaking of that searing anguish that was, for so long, a physical pain in her chest and throat.

This threw Harry into confusion. "I see. Sorry."

"I'm getting used to it, slowly. Eight years older than me, he was, but still so young. It was so unfair." She was momentarily angry, then continued after a moment's silence. "You? Do you work in town?"

"Oh no." He smiled at the idea and shook his head. "No, not me." There was another silence for a moment, and then Harry appeared to collect himself. "Mainly working at Moondreams House out at Waterthorpe."

"Oh, I know the place. Just out on an away-day, then?" Annie said. *He's not giving much*, she thought. This clearly wasn't a good idea.

Had he picked up her thoughts? "I'm sorry." He shook his head and blew out his cheeks. "I mustn't keep apologising, I know."

"Never mind. Let's just drink our tea, and then I must get my bus."

Harry took a deep breath. "It's just that I seem to be at a bit of a crossroads. I may lose my job, my employer said. Not anything I've done. He's such a skinflint. He's talking of selling the house where I work. I've already lost my wife." He must have noticed Annie's expression of confusion and concern. "Oh no! She's still around. I didn't mean … not like…" He paused. "To someone younger, I mean. My fault … after what happened. A bit of a loser, all around." He pursed his lips and looked down at his fingers.

Annie sipped her tea. *I wonder what he did*, she wondered. *Cheated, I suppose. Well, if that's the case, he deserved her going.* As she peeped at him over the rim of her mug, her natural empathy kicked in. He and she were the same age, but now he looked years older. She had a few extra pounds, but he hadn't worn well at all. "What is it, Harry?" She spoke softly. While she waited, she unwrapped the chocolate biscuit he had bought for her along with the tea. A kind thought. "Here, have this. We all make mistakes." She held it out to him and unwrapped the other that sat next to his mug. "Chocolate always makes a problem seem easier to cope with."

He looked up and a smile played at the corners of his mouth … and there was that dimple and the eyes as blue as a robin's egg. The memories came flooding back so hard that Annie had to take a deep breath.

CHAPTER 2

Annie stood at the sink, a cloth in one hand and a plate in the other. She stared out at her tiny garden. All the scabby grass and mud had been replaced with an artificial lawn and looked very green. The roses needed deadheading, and while the geraniums were a glorious shade of vermillion, the hosta that shared their trough looked slug-bitten. She was determined to try and do something about that. It was satisfying to see her hard work from last year was paying off. The cornflowers, her favourite, were waving gently in the sun. The blue, so piercing. Oh! That blue. Those blue eyes.

Annie was overwhelmed, yet again, by the thoughts that consistently returned to yesterday. She had slept fitfully, even though the dreams were kept at bay. Every time she tossed and awoke, those blue eyes looked at her with their mix of sorrow and puzzlement. She started to replay the conversation with Harry when the front door thudded shut.

"Hiya!" a voice called from the hallway. Annie turned as Simon, her brother, came bursting into the kitchen. "Hello, darling. Raffa, get down," he added, shoving gently at the eager little dog that was jumping up to greet him.

"Rafferty, no," Annie added for good measure. "Get down. I really am trying to train him not to jump up, but he's so keen to see you."

He came to her. "Sis," he said as he kissed her cheek.

Annie studied his face with its designer stubble, and his hair with the perfect amount of gel to hold it in place. "What are you doing here at this time of the morning? Shouldn't you be on your way into the office?"

"I thought I'd pop by and see you. I told them I was seeing a client on my way in, so they're not expecting me yet. Anyway, all the senior accountants are having a meeting this morning. They won't miss me. Cup of tea going?"

Annie turned and picked up the kettle. *Mmm, here it comes … again*, she thought and sure enough, Si started.

"Have you thought about what I said, sis?"

"Darling, really, I will do but I've been busy."

"Doing what? Honestly, Annie, you'll have to decide. You can't go on like this. Your savings are dwindling by the week. You need to supplement your income, or you won't be able to keep up the payments even on this place, never mind feed yourself properly."

"I just need to decide what I'll do. I could get a job at Tesco, I suppose. I just haven't got round to it."

"Are you nervous? I could take you to the Job Centre. You never know, they might have something along the lines of what you did all those years ago, when you left school."

She let his inference about her age go. "What? A dance teacher? I doubt it. Not round here, anyway. Not since Just Dance closed."

"Shame you didn't take the owner up when she offered you first option on the business."

Annie retrieved two mugs from the cupboard. "You said that before. I was too young, and anyway I didn't need to. Rob was able to give me everything."

"All this reminiscing isn't solving your current problem, sis."

"God, you're so persistent. I'll sort something." Muscles tensed in Annie's neck and shoulders.

The silence stretched as they sat at the tiny kitchen table.

"I met someone yesterday. A guy I haven't seen since I was at school."

"Really? That was ages…"

"Don't even think it, Si, never mind say it! You may be seven years younger, but one day you'll be surprised how quickly time passes."

"Mm, you're right," he conceded. "So, who was this person?"

"His name's Harry. He looked and sounded a bit of a sorry state." She proceeded to give him a rundown of their brief meeting. Maybe sharing it would put the encounter to rest in her mind.

"Now, don't go taking on a lame duck. You can't afford that. Rob certainly wouldn't have welcomed that sort of person."

Annie sighed. This conversation was not going well. "Well, Rob's not here. Harry does not count as a lame duck, and I'll get my finances sorted out, so you don't need to worry. Isn't it time you got to work?" With that, she took his mug, poured the rest of the tea down the sink and with her back to him, she began to run the tap into the washing up bowl.

"Okay, okay. I surrender. I'll see you soon."

Without turning, she grasped the sink edge as she heard the front door open and close. Tears of anger and guilty sorrow sprung to her eyes.

Where had the last years gone? Simon had been her little brother. The longed-for one who had taken such an age to arrive, she knew now. She had been so full of anticipation, even at seven years of age.

Now, as soon as the door closed, she regretted her outburst. She would have to text her apology. All she craved were his reassuring arms around her shoulders. Since their parents had passed away in quick succession, followed by Rob, they'd been alone together.

Annie had loved the fact that Rob cared for her so much; that he took charge of things. Now she realised his toleration of her as a dance teacher was a tad patronising, but she still loved him. She hadn't kept it up for long after they'd married anyway. Rob's ability to organise everything was so like her father and Si seemed to have inherited that trait, too. Now as she was becoming more independent she guessed she was at fault for allowing it to happen all those years ago when her need for the man she loved was so overwhelming. She was trying hard to be more self-sufficient, and it really wasn't Si's job to take on the role of her organiser.

She groaned. *More than likely I'm overcompensating because I'm becoming more confident. I shouldn't be spiky with him when it's me who is developing and changing.*

If only Rob hadn't died quite so young. *He drove himself so hard, I guess a heart attack was the likely outcome*, Annie thought, *but he would never listen to me. Too much like his mother. She loved being a martyr.* Rob's dad had more sense — he was such a kind and lovely man. Annie reminded herself to phone him at some point.

The sound of the doorbell interrupted her thoughts. Through the frosted glass panel, she saw the comfortably voluminous outline of her friend Ginny.

"Hi," she said as she opened the door. "You're just what I need. Come on in."

"I saw Si's car leaving, so I guessed you might be in the mood. So come on, fess up already, as they say."

Annie couldn't help but laugh. Even though she was older than Annie, Ginny's turns of phrase reflected the fact that she had teenage children. "'Spill the beans' I'd say." She led her friend to the kitchen.

"You're so not 'down with the kids' like me," Ginny said. Making herself at home, she moved across to fill the kettle and gather mugs. "You sit. I'll make you a restorative. Tell all."

Annie told her friend about bumping into Harry, which raised an eyebrow but elicited no comment. She also confessed that she understood Si's point of view. "I do need work, but I couldn't admit to myself, never mind him, that he was right."

Ginny sat for several moments. "Maybe only partially. Don't be too quick to jump into a job you won't enjoy. Something will turn up. You never know, it might even involve this Harry."

Annie laughed, and a weight lifted from her mind. "I doubt that. But perhaps you're right. I'm not sure if waiting longer is simply more procrastination, though."

Lying in bed that night, Annie tossed. Ginny was a true friend, though they were complete opposites. Her expansive and colourful choices in clothing were the antithesis of Annie's carefully chosen matching outfits. Ginny had swept into the room dressed in crimson and sapphire, swagged and bowed, frilled and draped like a Victorian music hall. Her clothing emphasised her fulsome figure but her confidence oozed and enveloped Annie with comforting warmth. Ginny could not have a kinder heart and had been the friend to be relied upon when times had been unspeakably vile. She always knew when to be silent; when to offer her wisdom; when to drink tea and when to produce a much-needed bottle of wine.

Today, Ginny had counselled waiting until the next time Annie met Si in person before she spoke to him. "Don't run after him. *You* need to stand your ground and wait for what will undoubtedly arrive. *He* needs to know you are serious about deciding what *you* want to do. Grab that bravery you've shown before with both hands. Your future is glowing. Simply FR," she added as an afterthought.

"What? FR?"

"Come on, babe. FR, For Real." Ginny grinned. "How am I doing?"

"The kids will think you've lost your head."

They laughed together uproariously, as they so often did.

Annie's mind turned, again, to her meeting with Harry. *I wonder if I'll ever see him again*, she thought before sleep finally overtook her.

CHAPTER 3

The thought of Harry was still there when Annie awoke. He had looked broken and shabby. What on earth had happened to destroy the confident, good-looking young man he had been?

On top of this, she couldn't resist texting Si: *Sorry for my outburst. You are right, of course.*

The response came back an hour later but did not set her mind at rest: *Talk about it again soon.*

"Do you know what, Annie?" she said aloud to her dog. "You need to get a grip." She'd had enough of wafting about. "I've made excuses and avoided people, and there are things I could be doing that I've deliberately turned away from," she continued, still addressing Raffa. "Friends have left me. Probably fed up with me always saying 'no thanks'". A bolt of understanding hit her with force. "God, I've become *boring*."

Mortified, Annie ran upstairs to the bathroom mirror. A wraith peered back at her. Rob wouldn't have been attracted to this Annie. In a flash, she yearned for a new purpose.

I think I'll take my book back to the library and have a mooch around there, she thought. *Maybe I can find a book on starting a small business.* The sudden idea surprised her.

Half an hour later, Annie was at Ginny's house. Her friend answered the door, still wearing her dressing gown.

"Do you fancy a trip into town?" Annie asked. "I thought I'd get the bus. There's no hurry. I can wait while you get ready."

"I would have done," Ginny said, "but I've got to wait for the man to come and service the boiler. Time for a quick cuppa before you go?"

"Why not?"

"If you put the kettle on, I'll run up and throw some clothes on."

Annie had poured out two cups and was sitting at the kitchen table as she waited for her friend. She loved this place and had many memories of Ginny mopping her tears and dosing her with wine or tea at the time she had needed it most, her olive arms enveloping her like a duvet. In more recent times, when merriment had begun to return she had wobbled like a crème caramel clutching her stomach or patting her chest to catch her breath as she laughed.

The room wasn't tidy by any stretch of the imagination. It reflected its owner. A fruit bowl overflowed onto the side, which was already cluttered with a pile of letters, a food mixer, the latest juicer — probably unused but bought on a whim of diet mania — a phone charger, a make-up bag, a mirror and half a loaf of bread. The room smelled of toast.

Ginny reappeared. "So, what are you doing in town?"

"I thought I'd go to the library and then buy some new make-up."

"Talking of which, just look at that!" Ginny's chair scraped back and she snatched up the make-up bag and mirror from the worktop. "If I've told Ellie once… I've threatened to take it all away. She shouldn't be wearing much for school anyway, even in the sixth form." She laughed and shook her head at her daughter's habits. "You know what you should do?" Ginny continued.

Annie put her head on one side and frowned. What was coming now?

"You should try Partner."

"What? The dating app? You've got to be joking."

"Yeah. Ellie's just met a really nice lad."

"Ellie? She doesn't need the internet to find someone. They must be falling over themselves to get to her."

"She doesn't want anyone from school. Too much teasing involved, apparently."

"I'd be much too scared to use a dating app. Anyway, it's for people who can't find anyone."

"No, they all do it now. You're more likely to meet someone with similar interests. You get a choice and just swipe right if you see someone you fancy. If they fancy you back and swipe the same way, there you go … bingo. Then you arrange to meet in a popular place, a pub or whatever. You take yourself there and if you don't think it's going anywhere, well, you just go your own way, in your own transport whenever you are ready."

"I don't think I want another partner, anyway." Annie looked down. "To be honest, it seems like a betrayal. Rob was perfect for me. I loved him so much."

"Just a thought," Ginny replied gently.

Wandering through the beauty department at John Lewis, perfumes assailed Annie's senses. She hovered around the counters, unsure what to choose. Assistants approached her but drifted away as she wandered on.

Annie returned to the first brand she had seen and pondered. A young lady in a smart black suit, powdered and perfect, came across to her. "Can I help you?"

Annie's forehead and the corners of her mouth were tight. "I'm not sure what I want, but I need a change. I look rubbish."

The assistant showed her even, white teeth as she gave a natural chuckle. "Oh, I think we can help you out. Why don't you sit there?" She indicated a high stool next to Annie. "I can give you a quick makeover. Don't worry — I shan't gush, and there's no pressure to buy anything right now. After I've applied a new look, you can go away, have a coffee, look in the mirror in the toilets and decide if you like it or not. You don't look rubbish at all. You're so lucky to have high cheekbones and your eyes… We can do something there. They have a good shape and are a lovely colour. Not too much shadow. Maybe a light foundation and a little blusher."

Annie raised her eyebrows.

The young woman, whose name tag read Debs, touched Annie's arm lightly with her manicured fingers. "It won't be a thick blanket, just a little contouring." Debs put on a pristine white coat over her suit and fastened a protective cape around Annie.

"Let battle commence," Annie said.

All the way through, Debs explained what she was doing and why. There was a small oval mirror on the counter, and Annie watched as her transformation flourished. "You might want to shape your eyebrows a little. They're not too thick, but if you taper them here —" she stroked the area in question — "it would enhance the shape of your eyes."

"I used to pluck them years ago, when I was working."

"There are all sorts of products now that make it easier and quicker. You'd be amazed at the technology that has taken over from an old-fashioned pair of the wrong-sized tweezers," Debs said. When she had finished, she held up a mirror. "What do you think? I've not gone overboard, but you can see here and here that I've contoured and emphasised your natural bone structure."

"You're certainly an artist," Annie said.

"These are the products I've used, but there's no rush to buy. Like I said, go and walk around for a bit. Take your time." She laughed prettily. She was certainly good at her job.

Annie went straight up the escalator and found the ladies' toilets. She glanced at her reflection on her way into a cubicle, and then as she washed her hands she looked more closely. She didn't look bad. Different, but not bad. Perhaps she'd go to the library and watch people she passed to see if they stared at her.

Maybe she'd bump into Harry again. Not that she fancied him or anything. Those days were long gone. But she was sorry for him. Yes, that was what it was. He looked like he needed a friend, and so did she, if she was honest.

As Annie mooched in that general direction, she caught glimpses of herself in shopfronts, the bus shelter glass, a car window. Her face looked alright. Maybe a hair job would be next. Her cut was always reasonable, but highlights would disguise the few grey streaks that had appeared since Rob had died.

Annie passed through the library's double doors. Nobody stared. A lady at the counter looked at her over the top of her glasses and nodded. Annie smiled back, tucked her hair behind her ear and moved towards the business section, taking a circuitous route and looking around as she went. Several people glanced at her, but that was all. She lowered her shoulders and raised her head.

She didn't see Harry. And that was just as well, wasn't it? He had changed and didn't seem to be doing well. Si was right. The last thing she needed was to be propping up someone else.

Annie found three books on starting a small business. She was heading back to the desk to get them checked out when she spotted him. Harry was sprawling in a low padded chair, looking at a magazine. As she stopped to decide whether to approach or not, he shifted and glanced up. A smile lit his features.

Although she'd just decided she was better off not seeing him again, her heart jumped. She watched as he folded his long legs, struggled out of the chair, and came striding towards her.

"Hello," he said. "We don't meet for so many years and here we are, twice in no time at all."

Now covered in confusion, Annie returned his smile. He looked smarter. He'd had a decent shave and while he wore casual clothes, they looked newer, crisper. Instead of a crumpled T-shirt he was now dressed in a short-sleeved shirt with a proper collar, and his shoes had a shine that they'd lacked before.

"I see you've found some books," he said, gesturing.

"Yes. I came to return the book from before, so I had a quick scout round while I was here." He continued to stand and said nothing more. Hell, this was awkward. "I better get them checked out."

"Yes."

Harry made no move to say anything else, so Annie headed for the desk. Acutely aware of every sound, she heard no pursuing footsteps. As she waited her turn, she saw him standing alone, head down. She moved along the counter to speak to the librarian and when she looked again, he had vanished. Her breath caught in her throat. Was that disappointment or relief?

As she looked down, placing the books in the cloth tote she had dug out of her handbag, she was startled by Harry's voice behind her. "Cup of tea?" He avoided eye contact and was a little pink when she turned her head. She hesitated.

He took a step back and shrugged, drawing his lips in. He gave a tiny shrug of nonchalance, which belied his whole demeanour.

Annie answered without thinking. "That would be lovely. Thank you."

In the café, he indicated she should sit, although she offered to share in getting the drinks. Again, he bought a biscuit to go with the tea. "You said things are always better with chocolate."

"Yes, I did." She smiled.

"You look different."

She touched her cheek, feeling self-conscious. "I went into Lewis's and had a facial update. Does it look too much?"

"No, not at all. You look nice." It was his turn to be awkward and he looked down, clearing his throat. "So, what books did you get?" Now he sounded too jolly.

"I was going to investigate starting a small business. I used to teach dance, but at someone else's school. I must do something to supplement my income. My brother keeps telling me. I'm probably thinking rubbish, though. Honestly, I don't know the first thing about running a business."

"Dance? Well, that's different. You never know. Plenty of people have started something up with great success and surprised themselves."

"I'm into ballroom and Latin for ordinary people, rather than the full range for professional types. I'd like to bring dance to the general public, for socialising and exercise. I taught for some time when Just Dance was open here in town. I qualified as a teacher through the IDTA — that's the International Dance Teachers' Association."

"You're excited about it. You sounded quite fired up just then," Harry replied.

Annie regarded him. Harry's own expression showed interest and enthusiasm. "I suppose I did. There's so much more to it, though. I don't know anything about the business side. There're premises, insurance. Oh God, and money. Dealing with people's money and paying bills. Nightmare. I'm not sure where to start." The sinking in her stomach as she spoke brought back the reality of her idea. "I might take the books straight back. It's all nonsense."

"You'd need an accountant and that does cost, but they could save you money and see you through the financial side of things."

"My brother has just qualified as an accountant. That's why he keeps pestering me to find a job." Annie smiled. "I haven't taught for a while, but I kept up my membership and I've been to some of the conferences since I stopped teaching, just to keep in touch. That side I'd be able to do quite easily."

"There you are, then. Worth taking those books home and reading up."

"Thank you. Enough about me. What do you do? You suggested your job might be in danger when we last met."

"Hmm, yes. It's not grand. Not grand at all. I'm a caretaker, I suppose, although my job title is concierge. Not as posh as it sounds. That's why I can have some time to myself during the day. Not much else to do. There could be plenty, but the owner is so tight with his money that nothing happens when I point things out to him, so I come here sometimes. If I lose my job, I lose my flat too. That's the main problem." He looked down at his hands, then folded his arms and shrugged. "Oh well."

Defensive, Annie thought, and she leaned forward. "Tell me?"

"It's that great pile of a place out at Waterthorpe. Used to be Waterthorpe House, but the current owner's wife renamed it. A bit fanciful…"

"Moondreams House? How weird when your name is Harry Moon. It must have been fate for you to be there. I'd have thought it must be derelict by now, although I haven't been that way for a long time. We used to have a dog years ago, and we walked it by the river there. It looked run-down then."

"Thanks." He smiled in a half-hearted manner.

"Oh, I didn't mean…"

"No, you're right, of course. It's far too much for me on my own. Since my wife left, there's a woman who comes in to clean, and she does some cooking. David Troughton is the owner. Since his wife died about twenty years ago, he's become more and more reclusive. Grumpy old sod. Sorry."

Annie nodded. "Not offended, carry on."

"I had a couple of jobs after school, 'cos I was always going to take a year out. Went abroad for four months. Then I started there. I'd met my wife-to-be, so I didn't want to go away to college, in the end. Bit of a whirlwind. Should have known no good would come of it. David's as rich as Croesus, well, by my standards. He's certainly not short of a bob or two, anyway. He won't spend it, though. The house needs all sorts of things doing. I think he's given up, to be honest."

"He must be lonely, rattling around in such a big house on his own."

"Yes, he is, I dare say. I have a flat there, so we bump along together. No socialising for either of us. Too risky for me." He gave a self-conscious laugh, and Annie wondered why it was risky. She didn't know him well enough to ask.

Silence descended. Harry avoided her eyes again and Annie sipped her tea. She was left wondering what had been said to bring this distance when they had been chatting amiably.

They made small talk for a while before Annie said, "I better get home. The dog will need an outing."

"Oh, what have you got?"

"He's only small. A Jack Russell crossed with a poodle. His name's Rafferty, but I call him Raffa. I got him when I moved into this house. He's such good company. Looks a bit like a scruffy black floor mop."

"You could bring him over and we could walk him along the river. Didn't you say you used to do that?"

"Years and years ago, yes."

"Only if you want to. Just as friends. No hidden agenda," he added with evident haste. "You might be too busy, of course. I understand."

"No, no, I'd like to. Always good to have another friend," Annie said.

"Yes, absolutely."

They arranged for her to come the following week. Annie didn't want to appear too keen.

"If it's raining or something, I'll ring you, perhaps? I'd better have your number, Harry."

At least she had avoided giving him her contact details. He had changed and she had no idea what had passed or what he had done. If she chickened out, she could avoid meeting again quite easily.

CHAPTER 4

Harry sat and watched Annie go. As she pushed the door, she turned to give him a wave. She didn't look the same as she had back at school, but he had known her straight away. Later, as they'd chatted, he'd recognised a flutter of the emotions he'd experienced as a youth. She was vibrant, though not artificial. Her eyes were merry, and she laughed without guile.

He still remembered the dance they'd shared. As it had finished, he'd pressed his lips to hers. It was not the kiss he would have liked. He had been nervous, and it was too short.

The next day, he had gone to school full of anticipation, but when the other lads started baiting him, he knew no good could come of it.

"Did you get yer leg over, then?"

"How was she? Hot or what?"

"I bet 'e chickened out. I wouldn't have done. I'd 'ave…"

That last remark was never finished, as Harry gave the lad a hefty thump, earning a mixture of wrath and jeering from the small group. He knew then that any relationship with Annie was doomed.

Her friends had probably teased her, too. Romances within the confines of school were never successful.

They'd all left school the following term. Although he'd thought of her with longing ever since, he hadn't seen her again until this week.

He needed a drink. It was a bit early, but perhaps he would go to the bar in town later and meet up with the lads. The College Arms wasn't especially his scene, but it was always busy, and there was bound to be someone he could talk to. Many of the regulars called in on their way home from the offices. They weren't exactly friends, but they seemed to accept him.

He pushed through the crowd and when he reached the bar, he finally managed to order a pint of beer. As he turned, he held his glass high to avoid it being knocked. Then he spotted the group he knew.

"Hi, guys," he said, gulping from his glass.

"Still on the beer, Harry?" one of them said as he held up his wine glass.

"What have you guys been up to?" Harry asked.

"I was just telling them about a new account I've conned someone into taking out with us. A nice little bonus for me soon, I believe."

There was general guffawing, presumably at the story that Harry had missed.

"So, what have you been doing at that stately home you manage? Hobnobbing with the rich and famous?"

"Hardly. Can I get you all another?"

"Very decent of you." They each gave Harry their order.

Bloody hell, it's going to cost me a fortune, he thought as he turned and fought his way back to the bar. No one followed to help him carry. It took him an age to attract the attention of someone as he held out his card. Finally, he was served with the round of drinks on a tray.

When he got back to the small, round table by which they had all stood, his group of friends were nowhere to be seen. The crowd was thinning slowly, so Harry turned and scanned the rest of the area. Where were they? Perhaps they had found a seat on one of the leather studded benches around the room. The tray was getting heavy, so he nodded at the young people who were clustered around the table where he was certain his friends had been.

"Do you mind if I put this down? I had some friends here, but I can't see them."

"Sure," one of them said. He wore an office lanyard around his neck with the name Roger Wright written in bold black letters next to his image.

A pretty dark-haired woman said to another young man, "Did you see them go, Si? You saw this space and made a beeline for it."

He shrugged and shook his head. "I saw one of them giving you the eye, Steph," the man named Si said. "There's admiration and then there's being a right dick, leering the way he was."

"He's lucky I didn't see him," Roger Wright said and put his arm around Steph's shoulders.

Harry raised his eyes. He could guess which of his friends that would have been. He looked around the bar again but could see no sign of the group for whom he'd paid all that money on a round of drinks.

"I think they've gone, mate." Roger pursed his lips and looked glumly at Harry.

"Oh, well, time I went too," Harry said. There was no way he would stay here, now, and see the looks on these young people's faces. "Have a few drinks on me." Turning, he pushed his way towards the door before they could say anything else.

Annie watched Si as he sipped his coffee and wondered if he was happy. She hoped so, but there was no one special in his life and she couldn't help worrying about him since they were now on their own.

"So, what have you been doing in your spare time? You need to have a social life. All work and no play, it's not right, you know."

"I was out last night, as it happens," Si said. "A group of us went to the College Arms after work. Got a couple of free drinks out of it, too."

"How did you manage that?"

"Some poor sod was up at the bar buying a round, and while he was there his mates skedaddled. Maybe they got fed up with waiting, I don't know, but I overheard them say they were going on to the Mayfair. Left him with a tray of drinks."

"That sounds a bit mean."

"One of them said they ought to wait for him, but the others laughed and told him he was being soft and the guy at the bar was a boring loser anyway. So off they went. The guy came back with the drinks and left them with us before doing a runner himself. Embarrassed, I suppose."

"That's such a sad story. The poor man. He probably spent a fortune on the round, too."

"Rog called after him, but he scarpered so quickly he didn't hear, I guess. It was busy."

"He must have felt so let down. Not exactly friends, were they? Just taking advantage of his good nature."

"I suppose so, but why was he with them, anyway? He looked a bit older. Not their type, really. Must be a bit desperate to hang out with people like that, if that's the way they treat him." Si shrugged.

He'd never understand the desperate need for friends and acceptance that some people had to cope with, Annie reflected. Si was the sort who always had a crowd around him even if there was no one special yet. Her thoughts turned to Harry. She could imagine what Si described happening to him, and she hoped he wasn't the man in question.

CHAPTER 5

When Annie awoke on the morning of the walk, it was soft and clear. The sky was mother of pearl with pale blues and pink-tinged clouds. The birds welcomed the dawn with their riotous calling, starting with the twittering of robins and wrens, before the thrushes and then the finches joined in. She was grateful her mum had taught her all that.

As she greeted and fed the dog and made her usual scrappy breakfast of tea and a single piece of toast, she couldn't stop thinking of the morning ahead.

"Raffa, do you think we should go?" she asked the dog. "I haven't got the excuse of bad weather. I could say I've twisted my ankle or something."

Raffa regarded her with soulful eyes.

"We're just friends. There can't be any harm, surely."

See you at 11 at the weir, she texted to Harry. She didn't want to show up and find he couldn't make it, or worse, he'd forgotten.

She turned up the car radio as she made her way to Waterthorpe. There was little traffic on the country roads, and it wasn't far, so she opened the windows and sang along as the wind whipped her hair. She had clipped Raffa's lead to the seatbelt fixing and he lay beside her in contented bliss, sniffing the air.

As she pulled into the car park, Annie saw Harry straight away. He was standing beside an old-fashioned cycle and still had one of his trouser legs inside one sock to keep it from entangling in the chain. He looked lonely by himself, but he smiled when he saw Annie's car approach. He started to walk towards her and then clapped a hand to his head before bending down to remove his trouser leg from its casing. As he straightened up, she saw he was laughing at himself and her shoulders relaxed.

Raffa leaped out of the car at the first opportunity, and Annie bent to gather his lead.

"I wasn't sure if you'd come," Harry said.

"I wasn't certain myself, but to be perfectly honest, I don't have that many friends anymore and well…"

"I know what you mean. I know quite a few people — but not so well, I discovered recently."

Annie glanced at him, but he said nothing further. She thought of the story Si had told her about the guys at the College Arms. Perhaps it was a common thing for men to treat each other that way.

Harry collected his bike and pushed it with one hand. They walked side by side towards the bridge over the weir without speaking. When they reached the kissing gate on the far side, Harry lifted his bike over before they passed through in awkward silence. On the other side, he blurted out, "I thought we could walk across the fields here. When we get to the big house, perhaps you'd like to have a look around — inside, I mean. Can you let the dog off the lead here? There are no sheep around."

He's talking too much, Annie thought. She bent to unclip Raffa, who cavorted around them both before running ahead. They spoke of generalities for several minutes, keeping away from anything personal.

Annie took a deep breath and sighed. "What a glorious day," she said. "It's quite warm." She began to relax. Perhaps Harry did too. They stopped while he took off his jumper and tied it around his waist.

"I confess, I don't have many real friends." His voice was quiet, and he studied the ground as he walked, one hand in his trouser pocket, the other pushing his bike. "I was a bit let down the other night." He shrugged.

Annie turned cold but said nothing except, "Oh?"

"Yeah, I was out with a group of guys. I've met them several times and we've become, well… I bumped into them at the College Arms."

Annie waited for what she already knew.

Harry gave a small laugh. "Mmm, they left me with a tray of drinks. They had to leave in a hurry, I guess. One of them must have had an emergency or something."

She said nothing for several seconds but then decided there was no way she would confess she had heard this story. "Oh no. That's a shame. I'm the same. People were all around when Rob died, but gradually that tailed off. I refused some invitations. I think people were trying hard, but I didn't want to be the odd one at the dinner table or sitting opposite some stranger, trying to make small talk. They stopped asking in the end. I do have one particularly good friend. Do you remember Ginny Larkin? She's Ginny Featherstone now. She was a couple of years ahead of us at school."

"The name's familiar."

"It was a long time ago. She's on her own. Well, she has a teenage daughter and a son who's coming up to GCSEs. She's been there for me during all the dire times. Rob and I were so happy. After he died, I found it hard to understand how the rest of the world could carry on as if nothing had happened, when my part of it had vanished. All I wanted to do was to shut myself away. Ginny picked me up. She knew when I needed something and what. I couldn't have managed without her."

"You lose your joy, don't you? Feel guilty?"

Annie glanced up at him, nodding. "And you?"

His voice brightened a little as he ignored her question. "I bet you help her out too. Ginny, that is."

"Yes, I suppose so." She whistled for the dog, suddenly needing a distraction. "There's the house." She pointed across the field.

"Yes. Shall we head that way?"

"Mmm." Annie nodded determinedly.

"It needs a lot doing to it. If David sold up, I'm not sure what I'd do."

"Is that a real possibility?"

"I don't know. I was telling my sister, on the phone last night. He's talked about it for a while, but nothing's come of it yet. She said it's like the Sword of Damocles, and I suppose she's right. I'm never sure when it may fall. The house must be a huge expense, but he does have the money. It's almost like he can't stir himself from a depression."

"Where is your sister these days?" This seemed a safe topic.

"Down in Cornwall. In Penzance, so we don't meet often at all. She teaches literature at a sixth form there."

"Did you never think to join her in Cornwall?"

"No way. Much too far. It's hard work here, but I do love it. And it does mean I can take a few hours off when I need to, so it's very handy in that way."

The footpath they took from the gate across the fields arrived halfway along the curved driveway. Annie could see the house was far from derelict but probably needed a good overhaul. The stone was a golden cream, the midday sun casting warm light that camouflaged any imperfections. It could have been from a fairy story, with its conical-roofed tower at one side and its huge windows with rounded tops.

"It looks glorious," Annie whispered, tipping her head back. The crowning glory was the grey-brown roof of ancient and expensive Collyweston slates, the preferred material of older traditional properties, although it was black with algae in places.

"We need to get someone up there to get that off," Harry said, following her gaze. "Probably why we get leaks. It's a specialist job, though. Not something I can do. I keep telling David."

"How on earth could anyone pay to build something like this in the first place?"

"I know. The walls are almost as thick as my arm is long. The original owner in 1800 earned his money with sheep. The Lincoln Longwool, apparently. Quite rare now."

"Don't think I'd know one if I saw it," Annie said.

They crunched along the gravel, squashing some weeds, and went around to the side.

There was a door with peeling white paint. "Tradesman's entrance, I'm afraid," Harry said. "Apologies."

"None needed, but what about Raffa? He's a bit muddy after that puddle he went in."

"Oh dear, yes. Mrs M is the housekeeper. She might comment, even though her work isn't that thorough. Would he be happy over there? It used to be a stable block, but it's empty now. There are some old blankets he can use to lie on."

"He should be alright. He'll need a water bowl."

"No problem."

The dog settled and was happy to have a sleep after his boisterous walk, so Harry and Annie crossed the courtyard towards the house.

They entered a large kitchen. It was swelteringly warm because the Aga appeared to be blasting out heat, although there was no-one in the room and no pans on the top. Annie wasn't sure it smelled too good.

Harry noticed her wrinkling nose. "Mrs M isn't a brilliant cook, as well as skimping on the cleaning. She's a good enough soul, though."

A huge enamel butler's sink and a wooden draining board filled the wall where a window overlooked the courtyard they had just crossed. Tall, panelled cupboards painted cream and with cast iron handles occupied the walls either side of the range. Above, near the ceiling, hung an old-fashioned slatted airing rack with pulleys and a cord to raise and lower it.

"My mum used to call that a Sheila Maid." Annie pointed up to it. "My Gran had one."

The huge oak table had a pile of papers on it and several cup rings, although there were coasters there too.

"Let me show you the more interesting parts of the house." Harry led the way.

They passed a couple of small, dark rooms that Annie surmised were a boot room and a scullery when she peered through the open doorways. Beyond the kitchen, a narrow set of plain wooden stairs ascended at one end of a dark corridor next to another door, which was closed. Harry turned in the other direction and they emerged into an enormous, square hallway where floor-to-ceiling windows with rounded archway tops were draped with heavy red curtains. The sunlight streamed in, its glow radiating from the rich colours of the oak-panelled walls and dispersing any gloom. The room overlooked a lawn and a flowerbed to trees beyond. All around the high ceilings was ornate moulded plasterwork, and hanging from the centre was a heavy brass chandelier that was faded and dull with age. A large, empty fireplace on one wall had a white marble mantelshelf and a heavy gold-framed mirror above. There were more heavy-looking wooden panelled doors on either side. Annie looked around in wonder.

"Is this what's called a Turkey carpet?" Annie stepped gingerly across the vibrant rug, carefully avoiding the worn patches where the fine weave of the brown backing showed. Round the edges were a complex pattern of tiles.

"Yes. It would have been remarkable at one time, but as you see…" Harry shrugged. "Come and look through here, though. This could be so amazing."

On the far side of the hall, he opened one of the panelled doors and Annie was stunned at what she saw as she entered. The room was vast. "Was this a ballroom?"

"Yes. In its heyday it would have been used a lot, but it's not used at all now. When David's wife was alive, they had grand parties and dances in here. The chandeliers get a feather dusting, and that's about as much action as it sees."

"The floor is magnificent."

"Hardwood parquet. Oak. It's original."

Annie's toes and knees were twitching as she longed to waltz across the stately space. Rob had allowed her to teach him the basic steps of the main dances, but he'd always remained wooden, counting as he moved his feet rather than sensing the rhythm and being subsumed by it as she was. But she could dream, and the distance of time lent a rosy hue to her memories.

Ah … her throat closed, and she coughed as tears sprang, unguarded. She turned to survey the rest of the room, blinking.

The old magnificence was still there: the large fireplace; massive mirrors; floor-to-ceiling windows at the end; two-tiered white wooden benches along the length of one side. Above, two vast chandeliers hung like spiders' webs dripping and sparkling in an autumn dew. Then, in one corner, a giant patch of damp was creeping around the powder-blue ceiling. A result of neglect, she supposed. Such a shame.

"It's stunning," Annie said once she had recovered. "So sad that no-one sees it."

"Or uses it," Harry added.

"What's happening up there?"

"We had a bad leak last winter. Some slates cracked under all that snow. Didn't realise until it melted, and then we lost a couple in the strong wind that followed. David paid to replace the lost tiles, but it's bound to happen again. This whole part of the roof needs replacing. It's by far the worst. It's not as if the whole house would have to be done in one go, although he could easily afford it. This is a separate single story. Shall we go back to the kitchen? I could show you some of the upstairs, but it's incredibly scruffy. Only David and I use it, and there are brown stains on the ceilings up there too, but not as bad as this. Only my rooms have been updated because I did them myself." Then he added quietly, "I needed a change after I found myself on my own again. Needed it to be mine. Part of the coping process. Trying to get over what happened, what I did. Impossible, of course."

He sounded suddenly jolly, giving Annie no time to enquire what he meant. "Right, come along. I'll make us a cup of tea, and I bought some good biscuits."

As they sat in companionable silence in the kitchen, crunching chocolate biscuits and sipping tea, Annie heard footsteps in the corridor. Her nerves itched and she swallowed. The only other people in the house were David Troughton and Mrs M, weren't they? Mr Troughton, the recluse who sounded grumpy and wouldn't spend any of his fortune on restoring the original beauty of the house. Suddenly she was nervous. Should she remain seated? Should she stand?

"It's okay," Harry whispered.

Fleetingly, Annie smiled at him, grateful for his understanding.

David Troughton entered the kitchen. He was tall and slim to the point of looking skeletal, with thinning grey hair, sunken cheeks and piercing pale blue eyes. His thin lips were unsmiling, which added to Annie's nervousness and she leapt to her feet, almost knocking her chair over. However, she realised she didn't have anything to say and slunk back down in her seat.

"You must be Annie Ellis. Harry said you might come by." He nodded at her and that was that. He moved across to get a fine porcelain mug down from one of the cupboards, filled the kettle and made himself a cup of coffee, all in silence. Annie glanced at Harry. He didn't seem ill at ease. He was used to the silences after all these years, she supposed. She looked at David's stooped figure as he went about his task. His jacket seemed too large for his frame, and his trousers had that look of being hoisted by braces until the waist was under his armpits. She smiled internally at what Rob would have said and the sideways look he would have given her.

"Harry showed me your ballroom. It's stunning."

"Hmm."

"Such a shame no-one else sees it anymore."

This earned her a silent look from the blue eyes. Annie lowered her own, but Harry jumped in to rescue her. "Annie used to be a dance teacher, so she was very impressed."

"Right." David finished his task and taking his mug, he headed for the door. "I'll leave you to it. Harry, when you're done here perhaps you would sort out that loose lock on the front door before it comes right off."

"Yes. I noticed it yesterday and it's on my list. Will do."

They continued to sit in silence until the footsteps had receded once more. "He's scary," Annie could not resist saying in quiet tones.

"Oh, he's alright. Very shy, of course. When his wife was alive, they had a vibrant, lively group here quite often. Jane, her name was. Everyone liked her. She had one of those outgoing personalities that people respond to, and he relied on her totally. He's been lost since then and receded into his own space. Bit sad, really."

"And you? Have you receded into your own space here too?" Annie asked. "Sorry. None of my business. It's just that I'm frightened of doing that since Rob died. Ginny said I should get out more."

"That's alright. Yes, I have been in a bit of a state. Things were difficult, but meeting you again has made a difference." Pink crept around his ears and across his cheeks, and he looked away.

Thrown into confusion, Annie said, "Thank you. It's always good to have friends." She stood. "I really better be going. Raffa will want his snack."

"Yes, of course. I'll walk back to the weir with you."

"Oh no. It's not far. I have Raffa, and you need to go and sort out wobbly door locks. Thanks for a lovely time."

She marched to the door, opened it and strode across the yard to collect the dog, who was still very sleepy on his pile of blankets. He looked up blearily.

"Come along. Another walk for you." Clipping on his lead, she waved at Harry, who stood outside the kitchen door with his hands by his sides and shoulders slumped.

"Bye," he called.

Annie was down the drive and through the smaller wrought iron gate before she thought consciously about her hasty exit. So speedy had she been, that they hadn't made a further arrangement to meet. Was that why he looked disconsolate at her departure? Oh well. She had his number, and she supposed he must have hers now because she'd texted him earlier. That was foolish. Too late now. *It does throw the ball into his court*, she thought. *If he doesn't want to continue this friendship, then fair enough. If he's looking for more, then that's tough. I'm not up for a relationship.*

As she strolled across the stubby grass, she reflected further on the afternoon. It *had* been very enjoyable.

For months after Rob's death, she had cried every day. Time had stretched ahead in empty darkness. It had been all she could do to get dressed in the morning sometimes. She hadn't cared about anything. People's attempts to include her had seemed trite and sentimental, and she had thrown their efforts back at them until they'd stopped trying.

Then the day had come when she'd realised she had to do something. Ginny had helped. She had stood by her, despite Annie's efforts to distance herself. It had been she who had given Annie a firm talking-to.

"One day, there will be joy again in being alive, the wind will sing, the sunshine will dazzle again, and you will shine in its light. Rob will always be with you and you will dance again, but only if you forgive yourself."

"What do you mean, forgive myself?" Annie had sounded aggrieved at the criticism.

"For still being here when Rob is not. Physically, I mean. You're experiencing guilt. That's causing depression. It's normal, but you can still enjoy what's left if you let yourself. It won't take away what you had before. It's another step. A different direction. That's all."

But Annie didn't want to make this thing with Harry more than a friendship. Still lurking at the back of her mind was that insidious fear: the one that told her if she fell in love again and found too much joy in it, somehow the precious love she had for Rob would be diminished, and her memories of him would be demeaned.

CHAPTER 6

That evening, Annie had an early shower and plodded around the kitchen in her slippers and pyjamas as she made a cup of hot chocolate. She took her drink into the sitting room and sank into the cosy armchair. Raffa padded behind and settled beside her. She reached over the arm and caressed his ear.

"Faithful boy," she addressed him.

Rob had been eight years her senior and when they'd married, he'd seemed so wise and worldly. Annie had loved him to distraction and had desperately wanted to have his child. But as the years passed, no baby arrived. She never experienced the exhilaration of a tiny hand, so complete and perfect, clutching her thumb in a vice-like grip. She watched her friends in hopeless anxiety. She adored Rob as she had never adored another being, and she had turned to an occupation that he had encouraged. He had pampered her through her training and indulged her through her teaching years.

He was her and she was him. She had wanted a family but that was never to be now. As she idly pulled Raffa's ears, she experienced the ache yet again.

The books from the library eyed her accusingly from the coffee table. She sighed.

"Oh, all right," she said aloud and picked up the top one. "I better look, Raffa, even if it's not going anywhere." She studied the spine. *Build Your Business*, it stated. She pulled a face and picked up another. *Business for Beginners*. She opened it to look at the contents. The first chapter almost put her off: 'Sole Trader or Limited Company'.

"Do I really want to be bothered to know what that means?" she asked Raffa.

Raffa's tail gave another swish on the wooden floor.

The next chapter wasn't so scary. Annie had sized up the competition already. There was only one group of older people who met fortnightly for a sequence tea dance session at the community hall. There appeared to be no other dance school for miles. 'Target Audience' came next, then 'Paying Yourself'. Ah, this was more interesting. She settled down to read. The words under 'Business Name', and then subsequent chapters flew past, and she reached the end of the little book before she knew it.

"I better tackle this first chapter, then," she said to the dog, who was now snoring gently. She flicked back to the beginning.

Annie took the second book to bed with her, along with a notebook and pencil. She was soon well into marketing principles and even learned what a USP was: a Unique Sales Proposition.

The clock moved silently until Annie glanced at it with stinging eyes. *Good grief! I better carry on tomorrow.*

But she couldn't sleep. She had no nightmares, and thoughts of Harry had fled, but she pondered over a name for her business. It rolled around and around in her head as she tossed and turned. Something catchy that reflected what she was going to do. It had to be something that let people know straight away that they would have fun, get fit, make friends, and learn a new skill.

The Sweat Spot? Oh no, that sounds gross. Moves and Grooves? No, it's not going to be that kind of dancing. More ballroom and Latin than hip-hop and street dance. eMotion Dance might be a possibility. It's sounds modern and vibrant.

Annie must have drifted off, because the next thing she knew the birds were singing again.

Leaping out of bed and flinging open the window, she sniffed at the morning air and surveyed the riotous profusion of colour in her neighbour's garden. The old boy had a way with plants, that was for sure. The ruffles of petals looked like a Monet painting with dabs of crimson, fiery orange, scarlet and vermillion. Her little plot was coming on, but it was no match for that.

She pulled on her dressing gown and capered down the stairs. Her heart was light, and her feet were skimming.

"Morning, Raffa. Such a beautiful day. Earth Dance Moon Dreams Academy?" she suggested, thinking of the dreams she'd had as a child. "Or do we prefer eMotion Dance Academy? What do you think? I know, what about eMotion Moon Dreams Dance School? I like it, but is it too much of a mouthful?" She picked up a tea towel, and holding it by the corners she began a Viennese waltz around the kitchen table, singing 'Oh What a Beautiful Morning' from *Oklahoma!* as she revolved.

Accompanying her morning cup of tea was the third of the books she had picked up at the library. This one was more about the business side of things, but she opened it with determination. She was ready for all that it could throw at her now. She read about staff and public liability insurance, business banking, marketing and finding an accountant. Of course, there was Si for that. She read about writing a business plan, although she didn't envisage a loan from the bank at this point. Still, it would be good to have one and present it to Si as a fait accompli. He would see she was serious and, above all, capable.

Excitement bubbled in her blood and made her breathless. After years of playing second fiddle to Rob, much as she adored him, and months of procrastination and hiding herself away, perhaps this was going to be her success, hers alone. She squeezed her shoulders up and clenched her fists under her chin before relaxing and letting out a sigh of air.

"I'm going to go for it," Annie said to Ginny later that day.

"I can see you may be finding your feet again. And does Mr Harry Moon have anything to do with this new-found sparkle in your eyes?"

"Oh, Ginny, honestly. No! He does not. I did see him again and we went to the big house and had a cup of tea. He's only a friend. And guess what?"

"I haven't the slightest idea." Ginny frowned. "You won the lottery? How about you met a gnome who granted you three wishes?" She paused. "I know, you're pregnant?"

Annie laughed. "Ginny for goodness' sake." If she hadn't been in such a positive mood, that last comment could have floored her, but she put those thoughts back in their box. "I met David."

"Who?"

"David Troughton, the owner of the house."

"Blimey, old Troutface."

Annie smiled. The nickname did conjure up a vivid image of the sour expressions she had witnessed. "I admit he was a bit scary. Do you know him, then?"

"I wouldn't say 'know', but years ago he supported our Women's Institute when we were trying to raise money for the new toilets. His wife had been a member. He wasn't quite such a recluse then, but you could see he might easily go down that route. She had just died, and he was very dour. But then that was understandable, and everyone tried to manoeuvre around him. He got worse, and now he's hardly seen around at all."

"Harry showed me around the downstairs of the house. There's some phenomenal period décor. Really beautiful. It's such a shame. It's slowly going to ruin. Poor old Harry can hardly cope on his own, and the old boy is too much of a skinflint to spend money where it's needed. Anyway, listen. This is not why I came round. I've got a plan. I need your views before I share it with Si."

"Go on."

Annie shared her idea of starting a dance school and some of her research. "What do you think? Is it a pie in the sky?" She knew she could rely on Ginny for honesty, and there was silence for several seconds. Annie realised she was holding her breath before she exploded, "It *is* ridiculous, isn't it?"

"It does sound scary to me, because I am a scatterbrain. You can make this a real hit, though. There's nothing else like it in this area, as far as I know."

"I've started to write down my ideas before I show them to Si. I need him to think well of it. I'm frightened he'll think it's stupid; that I'm stupid."

"He won't if you look professional and sound like you mean it. See if you can come up with some realistic pricing. Look on the internet at similar ventures elsewhere. Phone around and see what they charge. Make out you are a potential customer. They'll tell you then."

"Really? Do you think I could?"

"Of course. You can be quite anonymous and just say upfront it's a general enquiry. I'll do it otherwise. You need some accurate ideas of what you'd charge, so you need an idea of premises costs against what fees you would need to ask. There's the village hall, or that place where they do yoga and fitness. Unless that wouldn't be big enough. Hey, how about the community hall on the Park Estate? That's got folding doors, so it makes one big room. I saw it when I went to the Christmas Craft Fair. It's a shame the school is a bus ride away. They must have a hall."

"To be honest, the village hall floor is rubbish for what we'd need. The floorboards are too old and uneven. The knot holes and gaps are made for dancing shoe heels to get stuck. It needs to be somewhere with a decent laminate, even if it's not a proper sprung floor."

"See, you do know what you're talking about with the technical stuff. You must get an idea of prices, though, and the number of students you'd need to make it pay. Will you take children?"

"Oh, heck. That's a whole new thing. I would know what to do, but I couldn't cope with that to start. Maybe later. There's so much to think about."

Ginny stood up. "Come on, away with you. Go home and start making more notes, then get on the phone. You can do it."

The rest of the day disappeared as Annie continued to work on her laptop. Both her trash folder and her notes folder grew larger. By the time she went to bed, she was exhausted, and her eyes were prickly. She lay with the curtains pulled back and the window wide open, so that she would have the full reward of the night. The smell of warm earth and flowers drifted in. The moon was only a crescent and sailed somewhere at the front of the house, and she could see the stars with clarity. She looked until her lids grew heavy. Just before drifting off, she was transported back to one of her happiest memories.

Rob looked up at her across his plate of Züri-Gschnätzlets with its rich creamy sauce, then across to the Patscherkofel to the left of where she sat, with the westerly sun touching the tops of the mountain. A small smile played around his lips. Annie turned in her seat to see what he stared at. The rich mandarin glow made it seem deceptively warm up there. It was beautiful, and she melted inside as Rob turned back and captured her gaze. His eyes were deep and dark as they returned her desire. She cherished the small lines at their corners and the smattering of grey through his hair. She knew every contour of his face and body; the feel of it under her hands; his chin after a day's work, when pale stubble began to show. She knew every facial expression: the way his tongue poked the inside of his cheek when he was concentrating; the frown lines across his forehead and between his eyes when he was unhappy; the cheeky grin just before he said something teasing. They were all beloved. She was confident he would always take care of her and cherish her. He would never let her down.

"I shall remember this moment for the rest of my life," he said. "Balmy air, an amazing view, good food, and a beautiful woman. What more could a man desire?"

"Not in that order, I hope." Annie smiled at him.

He stretched across the crisp white cloth and took her hand, stroking the back of it with his thumb. "I saved the best 'til last, of course." They drank their wine and ate their meal in silence, speechless in the presence of such wonder. Every so often, she glanced at him. Sometimes he caught her looking and returned her expressions of love. At other times he was pensive in the vicinity of such magnificence, she guessed.

"What's that quote?" Annie asked. "*A thing of beauty is a joy for ever. / Its loveliness increases; it will never / Pass into nothingness…*"

"I've no idea," Rob said. "You're the artistic one, but it sounds very true."

"John Keats, I think," she said.

Later that evening, as the sun crept away they ran up the steps into the hotel, laughing and light. It was built into the hillside, so they left the upstairs corridor again through the full-length window halfway up the next flight of stairs. They then climbed the hill behind, using the moonlight to guide them. Finding a depression away from the rough-trodden path, Rob spread his jacket and they lay together. His arms were around her and her head rested in the familiar hollow of his shoulder. The night was secret and mysterious and spectacular. Gazing in wonder at a million stars, they lay in soft silence. Then he turned his head and she reached up to accept the gentleness of his lips. When remembered a month later, their loving that night was something that drove Annie distraught, near to madness.

After Rob died so suddenly, she was devoid of all feeling at first, hardly believing what had happened. She moved like an automaton through the procedures of gaining certificates and booking a church and caterer. Then her anger at him for leaving her took over. How was she to manage? She had no idea about running a house, with its bills and complications. This was followed by overwhelming guilt that she could do nothing about it, and it hadn't been her that had died. She was here and he was not. He didn't deserve to leave this life and all the promise it held.

Annie never admitted to anyone the thing she had done next. The night she went out was chill and blustery. She didn't care. She didn't mind if she caught a chill and died too, such was her depression. Even Si didn't understand her grief, although his own for her was real enough. He was still too immature to fully cope with her. She simply didn't care about herself.

She did remember to put on a coat over her pyjamas before sidling along the hedge and up the road, her slippers making a soft padding sound. The wind thrashed the trees on the other side and a pile of leaves swished around as she hurried on.

At the lychgate she hesitated but was beyond caring, so she passed under it. In the cast of a streetlight, she noted the last fragile rose petals strewn on the dark iron earth. Even they were dying. Slowing her pace, she passed all the old, lichened headstones standing at wonky angles. Only sparing a glance at the tiny graves of Victorian children, she passed the newer black marble and shiny grey crosses before she reached the far corner, where she stopped by the now familiar patch. It looked different in the shadows as the moon came and then disappeared behind clouds again. She stood still, unsure what to do now she was here. This crushing weight that she dragged around day after day was relentless. The anger and guilt had dissipated, leaving a dark empty space where she didn't care about anything: not her appearance, nor her safety, nor the ministrations of her few friends.

She crumpled onto the grass, head hanging like a lead lump.

When she awoke, she was lying next to her husband's grave, wondering how she'd got there and not knowing how long it had been. With a creeping awareness, she realised she was very cold. Her clothes were damp. It was still dark, but she had no idea of the time. As she sat up and brushed her fingers through her hair, a dried leaf fell to the ground next to her. She picked it up and looked at it with puzzlement.

As Annie lay in her warm bed remembering the state she had been in then, she marvelled that she had come through the worst of it without greater penalty to herself. Ginny had responded to her knock on the door, even though it was two in the morning. Friendship and hot chocolate had proved her saviour. Ginny hadn't asked and Annie hadn't told her why she was out or where she had been. Ginny's soft arms had encircled her friend and Annie had shrunk into the comfort.

From that moment, Annie had been determined to start living again. As she'd placed the fragile brown leaf in an empty necklace box, it had become a symbol. The dried and dead thing was boxed away. She would watch out for the pale green shoots of spring. She had relapsed sometimes, but never to that extent. The box remained buried at the bottom of her underwear drawer, out of sight and gradually forgotten.

CHAPTER 7

Si seemed to take ages studying all Annie's notes and her business plan. He frowned. He clicked his tongue. His lips pursed, and Annie became more and more anxious for a response. With extreme discipline, she kept her mouth firmly buttoned before observing him nodding sagely.

In the end, she simply could not resist saying, "I'd need your support, especially in the accounting department. Do you think it's plausible? I don't want to make a complete train wreck of it."

"This might seem terrifying, but it could be the most marvellous thing you've ever done," Si said. Then he seemed to think better of his choice of words. "Well … not terrifying, but challenging. Is this really what you want to do? There may not be much money in it for a while, but there could be enough to tide you over without completely using all your savings. I do think it could make you a living wage."

Annie let her breath out in a gust and her shoulders relaxed. She didn't realise she'd been so tense.

"I'm sure it could work," Si said. "You have the skills and the ideas by the look of this. It's very thorough." He lifted her document. "What about a venue?"

"I've been to see a couple. One was too small. The floor of the other was hopeless. I'm going to see the community centre on the Park Estate tomorrow."

"Where did you get all this information, about insurance and all the rest?"

"I got some books from the library."

"I have to say, you seem to have been doing lots of research, and you've come up with a plausible plan, sis. I'm impressed."

"Thank you, it's taken me quite a while. I wanted it to be right before you read it. Do you really think it's possible?" she asked again. Still she was in a tizzy, lurching from excitement to lack of confidence in her plans.

"Annie, it is," Si said.

Annie launched herself at him and gave him an enveloping hug. "Thank you, Si. That means so much to me. You have no idea."

"You'll need to take it slowly at first, I would think. Build it up in small steps. Get people's confidence. I think you could end up making quite a good living out of it. What about all this marketing you've written about? You'll need a budget for that eventually."

"You're right, but I can start off with social media. I might ask Ginny's Ellie to check it through with me, but maybe when I've got the dance school going, it'll be easier. I'll need a website. That could cost quite a bit."

"One of my mates can do that. He did one for his sister's nail business. Rog Wright? You've heard me talk about him."

"Oh yes. That would be great."

"You can tell him what you want, and he'll do it well, I know. It would cost something, but I think he'd do it cheaper for a favour. He owes me. I got him hooked up with Steph Harris, since he was mooning over her for ages."

"Si, honestly." Annie laughed.

Si turned to the sink to put his mug in the bowl and stood looking out of the window. "So, what about this guy you met? You haven't mentioned him." He seemed to be avoiding eye contact, after the tension of their last conversation about Harry.

"We met again some days ago, but I haven't seen him since. We only went for a walk. I took Raffa. It was lovely by the river. Oh, and he showed me around that great big place, Moondreams House in the village. He works there as a concierge. Caretaker really, I think." Was she babbling? "I've been too busy. Honestly, he's just someone I used to know a long time ago. He's got some complications from the past, I think. I'm sure you're right. I probably wouldn't call him a lame duck or a loser, but I'm not on the lookout for anything more. Rob was my world, Si. Now it's just you and me. Us against the world, little brother." She went and wrapped her arms around his waist, her head resting against his spine. He turned to face her and enfolded her in a hug. "Thank you," she muttered.

"Nothing to thank me for. You've done all the hard work. You can do it and of course, I'll help in any way I can. So long as you don't expect me to come along and actually dance!"

Annie rang the guy who looked after the community centre and arranged to meet him at the venue, so she could give it the once over. It was a grey, drizzly morning. She skittered from her car to the front entrance, leaping across a puddle on the tarmac, and pushed open the sturdy wooden door. A beechwood coffee table with various pamphlets arranged artistically stood on a red rug in the middle of the foyer, and on the far side was a matching desk and a counter. It all looked very smart.

Annie entered the ladies' toilet and sniffed the air. It seemed alright. Tentatively she approached the door labelled 'kitchen' and stuck her head in. It looked well equipped and smelled of stainless-steel spray cleaner. A set of double doors to one side of the counter were the only doors left. The corridor on the other side was dark but as she stepped through, lights came on automatically.

"Hello," she called. "Hello! Mr Jones, are you there?"

She heard a clunk and a swear word, so she headed towards it.

Pushing another door, she saw the man in question, on his knees and mopping up water that had presumably come from the bucket at his side. "Be right there," he said.

Annie stood and waited, taking the opportunity to take in her surroundings. No 1970s orange and brown here. The floor-to-ceiling curtains were very tasteful, in pale greys and shadowy pinks. Modern double-glazed windows all along one side looked out onto a wide area of green. She tipped her head right back to observe the ceiling, which soared above her in sweeping triangles and swooped back down to meet cream-coloured walls. The floor was amazing. She flexed her knees and bounced gently. It was sprung, and she could imagine gliding across it like a ship in full sail. Then she smiled at her own vision. Those days were in the past, but this would make a splendid area for beginners.

Mr Jones stood up with a good deal of huffing and puffing. He strolled towards her. "Mrs Ellis?"

"Yes. It's a marvellous place, this," she said. "I'd love to have my classes here, but have you a price list, please?"

"Yes, if you'd follow me. We've got all the usual facilities." He rattled off various kitchen items, toilets, and many others too numerous for Annie to take in. "We have staging too," he finished.

"Right," she said. "Sounds wonderful." He marched ahead of her, leaving the door to swing behind him. She managed to catch it and scuttled after him.

He entered an office with a desk upon which papers were piled high. "Right, where are we?" He rifled through several piles before dredging up a folder. Opening it, he handed her a list. "Do you need to see the other facilities? Only I'll be locking up in ten minutes."

"Er, no. It all looks lovely. Thanks for this." She waved the paper at him. "I'll take it home and let you know if I want to proceed." She hoped she sounded professional.

"You'll need to be quick. We only have Tuesday evenings free."

Back at home, sitting at the kitchen table with the list in front of her, Annie was mortified. The prices quoted for the community centre were outrageous, even with a reduction for residents of the estate, which she was not.

"Oh, Raffa, what am I going to do now? There's nowhere else."

She couldn't let her vision evaporate so soon. But where else could she go? If she went further afield, into the city, for example, it wouldn't be for local people, and anyway there would be more competition from towns on the other side. She put her head in her hands. Her thoughts were interrupted by her phone buzzing.

"Go away. I don't need you now," she said to the ether. When it stopped, she was relieved until it started again almost straight away.

Perhaps it's something serious, she conceded, and she reached across to answer it without looking at the screen. Her mind was still elsewhere. "Yes, who is it, please?"

"Oh dear. Have I called at a bad time?" asked the disembodied voice of Harry.

Annie closed her eyes and opened them again, determined to answer in a better frame of mind. "Sorry, Harry. No, it's fine."

"It's a while since we met. I wondered if you'd like to do it again. As friends, of course. Perhaps we could go for a coffee and a stroll in the country park as a change of scenery."

No harm in that, Annie thought. *Just as friends*. "Why not?" she said. "Maybe in a day or two, when this awful wet weather has passed." They planned an outing and Annie said, "See you on Wednesday, then," before cutting the call.

She resumed her introspection until, with a sigh, she arose to put the kettle on. At that moment, an idea smacked her in the face. Moondreams House. The ballroom. Why not? It wasn't far away from the estate and the village. Okay, it would be a car ride in the evenings or during the winter, but there was room to park. The size of it was great, and the floor was perfect.

Why not indeed? And then Annie suddenly remembered David Troughton. It was his house, and by repute he was virtually a hermit. Hell's teeth, would he even hear her out?

CHAPTER 8

By Wednesday, the sun had returned. The grass was fresh and green, and several birds were giving vent to their feelings about the general balminess of the day. Annie was almost bursting to ask Harry what he thought of her plans to talk to David about using his ballroom. She would need to pick the right moment to approach David, though, or the idea would go the way of the others. It was almost a last resort. She was quiet as she and Harry strolled, aware of his sideways glances. As they wandered along the tarmac path, Raffa cavorted, happily ignoring the water birds that bobbed on the lake.

"Is everything alright?" Harry asked.

"Yes, absolutely." Annie made an effort and remarked on the weather, but her mind was elsewhere.

"I am sorry if you're not in the mood for this outing."

"No, it's me who's sorry, Harry. Look, can we sit for a moment? There's something I want to ask you."

"Yes, of course. Er … right." He appeared to be thrown into confusion, but moved towards a bench overlooking the lake.

Annie clipped on Raffa's lead and hooked the end over one of the bench slats. She needed to concentrate. *He must be wondering what's coming*, she thought.

Harry stared straight ahead, with his fingers linked between his knees. "If it's a problem … meeting me every now and again…"

Annie took a deep breath. "No. No, it's not that at all." She turned and looked at him, although he was avoiding her gaze. "The thing is … I'm looking for somewhere to set up a new business. Quite a small concern to start with."

"That's good. I'm sure it'll be good for you in all sorts of ways," Harry said. "You always were a smart one with plans. You've read those books then, have you?" He glanced sideways at her with a small frown still creasing his brow.

"Yes. I'm going to start a ballroom and Latin dance school but … well, I've run into a snag, and I haven't even started yet." She told him all about her ideas, her plans, her encouragement from Si — and her number one problem. "I can't find any suitable premises."

"I know you said you used to teach, but goodness me, I wasn't expecting that. But solving your problem is easy," Harry said. "Use our ballroom."

Annie's heart soared. "But what about David? It'll be the last thing he wants, won't it? People tramping through his house, noise, and music. It's such a wonderful room and would be perfect but … it's his private space." She grimaced and shrugged.

"We won't know until we ask him, will we? Don't put your umbrella up until it's raining, as my Dad used to say. Mind you, I've spent my life trying not to put mine up, as he advised, and then it pours, metaphorically speaking. Still, that's another story and my own fault." He turned his head away and took a deep breath.

"Oh, Harry." Annie put her hand on his arm and smiled at him with relief. She caught his expression as he looked at it and then back at her. "Thanks so much for your encouragement. It means a lot. I'll have to pluck up my courage and approach David as soon as possible." She hurriedly removed her hand. "Right," she said, jumping up. "Let's go for that cup of tea at the Watersports Centre." She nodded at its outline, built on stilts next to the lake.

Once they'd arrived, Annie sat opposite Harry with her hands around her mug and looked sideways at the water, blue in the sunshine and dappled with ripples of light. A lone sailing boat was out on the water and the youngsters were laughing. She remembered when she and Rob had done something similar, and the swoop she had experienced when she'd seen his legs in shorts for the first time. That was probably when she knew he was the one for her.

Annie glanced across at Harry. He was so different to Rob, and he might be scruffy-looking, but at least he ate with his mouth closed and his manners were faultless. He was kind and generous and seemed to understand her. She smiled wryly at her thoughts and as he glanced up, he caught her look and his hand stopped halfway to his mouth.

"What? What are you thinking?"

"Oh, I … nothing really. I was wondering about the ballroom idea," she lied.

"No time like the present. Let's go and talk to David now," Harry said.

"I don't know about that." Annie glanced down. "I'm not dressed for it, and I haven't thought about it clearly enough."

"Come on, Annie. I bet you've thought about nothing else for days, and David won't even look at what you're wearing. You can ask him and then I'll back you up. He won't hear any noise from his rooms at the other end of the house. We can park cars round the side, so he won't be aware of comings and goings. It'll be my responsibility to clean the place."

Annie noted his use of 'we'. Here was a new problem. "I hadn't considered your wages for that. Oh, how terrible. I'm so sorry. It'd be extra work for you."

"Let me be the judge of that. I'm sure we can come to some arrangement. Look, I don't know about you, but I'm excited at the prospect. It's what the place needs. Any little activity in the house will be good. When it takes off, it may make David realise he *has* to do something. I really do think it will stop everything slowly closing down and crumbling," he smiled, "including David."

Annie caught his mood and grinned. "It would need to be properly contracted and signed. This can't be some hole-in-the-corner thing."

"Absolutely. It'll be a proper business arrangement. You might need a solicitor to do that."

"I've got lettings documents from other places that weren't suitable, so they might be a basis for an agreement."

As Harry drove them in his car with Raffa safely in the back, they chatted about Annie's ideas. By the time they arrived, Harry knew almost as much as Annie did.

"Do you know what I think? It's bloody marvellous, that's what. Very impressive. I think this could be the saving of the house and us both too."

Annie was unsure if 'us both' meant him and David or her and him, but she didn't have time to wonder as they arrived outside the big house and he leapt out of the car. She didn't even have time to gather herself together before he opened her door with a flourish. Here was a glimpse of the Harry he had been at school: dynamic, always on the go, popular with everyone and charming, too.

"Shall I put Raffa in the old stables again?"

That having been achieved, they entered the house by the same door as before. Harry tossed his keys onto the worktop and beckoned for her to follow him. He seemed invigorated while she was nervous, extremely nervous.

Once they reached the huge entrance hall, Harry said, "Wait here a minute. I'll go and dig him out."

"Harry, I'm not sure this is such a good idea," Annie said. "Maybe I'll go home and think about it some more."

"That's just procrastination. You know it is." He came to her, put his hand gently on her shoulder, lowered his chin and gave her a soft smile with his dimple showing. "Hey. It'll be fine. He might say no, but then you'll be no worse off than now."

Annie looked up at him and gave a small nod before he turned and left her, standing alone and quaking. She wasn't sure if that was because of Harry's gentle closeness. He had left an almost imperceptible waft of earth and paint and cologne. It wasn't Rob's smell, but it was comforting.

"David!" Harry called. "David, we have a visitor who wants to talk to you."

Annie shook herself from these mental ramblings. There was no turning back now. The house was silent apart from the odd creak of settling timbers in the early summer sunshine. Then she heard footsteps and swallowed. They came closer. A rotund lady waddled into the room, carrying a can of polish and a duster. Annie smiled at her.

"Hello, duck," the woman said in the local way. "Can I 'elp you?"

"Harry has gone to find Mr Troughton for me."

"Oh, David. 'E'll be in 'is rooms. You alright there, then? Anything I can do to 'elp?"

Annie declined the offer.

"I better get on, then. Got so much to do 'ere, and only me to do it all." She sighed and huffed as she continued towards the kitchen.

As Annie stood alone in the cavernous hall with the huge empty fireplace and her own image staring back at her from the massive mirror above it, she felt small once more.

More footsteps approached. Annie's palms were sweaty, and she rubbed them down her skirt.

Finally, a hand came around the leading edge of the door opposite, into the hall where she was standing. The tall, lean frame of David Troughton followed the hand and Harry shuffled in behind.

Annie took a deep breath.

"Good afternoon, Mrs Ellis." David stretched out his hand, and Annie was glad she'd wiped hers down.

"Please, it's Annie."

"I understand from Harry here that you have a proposition for me."

There was no ducking it now. "Yes, well…" She ground to a halt, feverishly thinking how best to phrase what she had to say.

Harry leapt in. "You want to start a small business, don't you?"

A look flitted across David's face, and she guessed he was imagining her asking for money.

Mortified, Annie scrambled on. "Years ago, I trained as a ballroom and Latin dance teacher. I've kept up my membership of the IDTA, although I haven't taught in years. Now I find myself on my own. My husband … my husband died a while ago." She gulped and blinked rapidly.

"I see. And IDTA?"

"Sorry." Annie grimaced. "It's the International Dance Teachers' Association. I took their exams and stuff. I've continued to pay my membership, so I still get all the guidance and dance notes for new sequences. There's an annual conference too. I haven't been recently, but I have quite often, in the past. My husband and I used to take a long weekend break so I could go. Then we'd spend the rest of the time exploring together. Sorry, I'm gabbling."

"Harry, perhaps you'd be kind enough to make a pot of tea. Mrs Ellis, Annie, shall we sit?" David indicated the way and they headed back down the dark corridor to the kitchen. There was no sign of the housekeeper. "Now, tell me how I am to help with this venture. Are you looking for investors?"

He looked and sounded like someone from a past era. A string vest showed through his white shirt. He also wore a jacket and tie, along with round-toed lace-ups. Did he dress like that each day, in his own house, when no visitors normally came? Had he quickly changed because she was here? It dawned on Annie that perhaps he was as nervous as she.

"Oh no, nothing like that. I should like to start a dance school. There isn't anything in this area. I've done my research. I have the backing of an accountant." She didn't admit it was her brother. "I need a room or a hall with a good floor that I can afford to hire. That's proving difficult. This dream can't evaporate before it's begun." Annie was begging despite herself. "I'd like to give lessons for ordinary people so they can meet friends, have fun, exercise and learn a new skill. I don't need money, just premises."

"I see." David sat back and folded his arms, surveying her with shrewd eyes.

Annie knew enough about body language to start feeling breathless. *Please don't turn me down before you've had time to consider,* she thought. She gulped some air and carried on. "I would pay you to hire your ballroom. We would be a small group, and we wouldn't bother you. Harry could open for us and clean, and I'd pay him, too. We wouldn't make a noise."

"There'd be music, presumably."

"I told Annie you wouldn't hear that since your rooms are on the other side of the house." Harry came to Annie's rescue.

"Yes, and it wouldn't be loud, raucous music anyway, not for the sort of dancing I'll be teaching."

"We would park cars around the side, so I'm sure you wouldn't hear those coming and going either," Harry added, which earned him a scathing look.

Annie leaned forward, willing him to say something positive.

"We better talk terms, then. I think there should be a trial period. If it's too much, we might need to reconsider."

"Yes, of course." She breathed out, long and slow. Did she dare to believe? She glimpsed Harry's face as he put the teapot down on the table. A smile flittered across his face and his dimple showed, but he assumed a more serious expression as David glanced at him.

"Three months would be quite adequate to see how it goes. I'm not at all sure this will work. I do *not* want people tramping everywhere and poking around. I do *not* want noise. I lead a quiet life. You can use the French doors that go straight into the ballroom. The path goes across the front and round to the courtyard, where you can park cars. If there's any revving of engines or slamming of car doors at all hours, then…"

"I assure you, I will respect your peace, Mr Troughton." Annie said this with a small degree of angry confidence.

"Mmm. What about payment? I have no idea about these things."

Aha! A weak spot, and he's admitted it, Annie thought. *Still, I'll not exploit it.*

"I'll ask a nominal amount," David continued before she could suggest an amount. "You can negotiate with Harry about his wages, but it's not to encroach on his work for me. If there's any damage, you must pay for it. I assume you'll be fully insured. I'll take five pounds an hour."

Her heart leaped. "I shall have full public liability insurance, as well as all the necessary indemnities. That's not very much rent, Mr Troughton. I was thinking eight pounds."

"Are you going into business? You'll pay a reasonable amount, but in bartering you are supposed to ask for less. I'm not a charity, though, you know. It'll be five pounds an hour for the first three months. After that, we'll re-negotiate." He said all this with not the smallest twinkle of a smile.

"Thank you so much." Annie beamed at him and then looked at Harry. "Thank you," she said again.

"Right, I'll take my tea and go to my rooms. I'll put it all in writing and send you a copy. Give your address to Harry. Sign it and return it. Oh, and let me know when you propose to start this thing. Good day, Mrs Ellis." They shook hands.

As he closed the door behind him, Annie plonked down in her chair. "That was like a whirlwind. I'm exhausted."

"But he's agreed." Harry sat down opposite her and topped up their mugs of tea. "That's marvellous."

"It's certainly a giant leap forward. I'm so grateful to you, Harry, for setting it up and pushing me to give it a go."

"To be honest, I didn't say, but I wasn't confident. He's such a hermit. He talks with me sometimes for quite long spells, but we've been leading this weird existence here together for years now. It suits us both, I think. He hardly sees anyone else. Even the shopping is delivered, and Mrs M does a bit of cooking."

"I met her just before you arrived back with Mr Troughton," Annie said. "He's certainly retreated now the business is done and out of the way. I shall have to make certain people don't stray from the set path between their cars and the ballroom, or we'll be dead in the water before the probationary period is up.

I feel quite nervous, but it's the only affordable option. I can hardly believe the price he's asking. Can we have another peek at the room?"

The way from the kitchen, through the vast entrance hall, to the ballroom was becoming familiar. Again, Annie looked around in awe. "Perhaps David might get that horrible brown stain removed, but I know I can't ask for more at the moment. I'm so happy." She clasped her fingers under her chin. "I want to take the image of it with me. We need to talk about your wages too, before I get carried away."

"How about for this probationary period, I'll do the cleaning for free? We can set a fee when you're up and running."

"Oh no, no." Annie didn't want to be in his debt. That could be so awkward.

"There won't be much to do until you have greater numbers," Harry added.

"No, Harry," she said with determination. "There'll still be dust and … and the toilets. I assume there are toilets. I should have checked."

"Yes, there are."

"Well then, we'll compromise. A nominal wage for the probationary time."

Harry grimaced but nodded. "You deserve this to work. You're clever and talented." His eyes slid away. "At the school discos, you stole the entire floor with your rhythm and style. You were always lovely."

Annie didn't know how to respond to that. Just friends, he'd said. Perhaps that was all it was.

CHAPTER 9

Annie paced as she awaited her first students. She was exceedingly nervous. She'd had several enquiries via her new website and social media outlets, but what if none of them turned up? Or only one? Well, she could dance with one person, but it wouldn't pay any bills. She grimaced at the thought. What if it was a total non-event? She was only offering a beginners' class to start, although none of the enquiries had been for more advanced classes, anyway. She could easily take on both of those if that's what people wanted. If someone contacted her to indicate they would like something more, it would be such a relief.

Harry had greeted her at the door and tried to look busy to start with. Now he was standing next to her, no longer pretending, but keeping her company. She was grateful for his distracting small talk, but her eyes kept straying to her watch. She set up her phone and linked it through the mixer to the speaker. Her music was ready. The microphone was waiting, although if only one or two turned up she wouldn't need it.

Wait! What was that? A car door — no, two doors.

She glanced at Harry, and he smiled back at her before gently squeezing her shoulder. "I'll leave you to get on." Then he leaned in and kissed her cheek. "You'll be great."

Annie didn't have time to consider Harry's action, nor did she watch as he walked away.

The French door to the garden path opened, and a young man in his mid-twenties stepped through, looking hesitant and taking in his surroundings with an expression of awe before he spotted Annie. She approached with a smile and an extended hand.

"Hi," the man said. "I'm Stephen. I've never done anything like this before." He grimaced.

"Welcome. It's good to meet you." Annie hoped to put him at his ease, despite her own nerves. "I know we exchanged several emails, so you'll remember it's half price for this first lesson. I know you said you'd done nothing like this before, so it's a taster session to see if it's for you."

"Do you remember I said I might be on my own? I thought my girlfriend would join me, but she's my ex now." He shrugged. He was younger than the average ballroom dancer, and his blue eyes were piercingly bright and mischievous. Annie thought he might add much to the class.

"Yes, I remember. It won't be a problem, I'm sure."

The door opened again, and a middle-aged couple came in. They each carried a small cloth bag. "We've brought our dance shoes." The man waved his bag.

"Marvellous. Have you danced before?" Annie asked.

"No, but I read up about it, and we went to that warehouse place in Spalford."

"I haven't got any special footwear." Stephen looked worried.

"Absolutely not necessary for this session. If you decide to keep coming, we can talk about dance shoes, but you don't need them to start." Annie turned to the couple. "Are you Christine and James?"

"Mmm. This room is amazing." Christine tipped her head back and regarded the space.

"I had no idea it was like this," her husband said. "I tried to find it on the internet because you had no pictures of it on your website. Only generic pictures of dancing."

Annie's stomach churned at the implied criticism. She would rectify that before she left tonight and use her phone to take some photos, as long as no one minded. A waft of fresh air announced someone else, and Annie's heart leaped with elation as a lady entered the hall. Possibly she was in her fifties, although it was hard to tell. She looked like Miss Marple.

"Good evening. My name is Edith Hill. I haven't danced before, but since my sister passed, I need to do something different and get out and about. I've spent much time nursing her and not pursuing my own interests." She sounded like a headmistress from the 1950s.

Annie took in the woman's long, flowered skirt, lilac jumper, and T-bar shoes. "Well, you're welcome here," she said.

As Stephen smiled at the newcomer, dimples appeared at the corners of his mouth and his eyes sparkled with suppressed amusement. Christine and James both nodded but kept to their own area.

Annie gave them each a form to fill in their details. Christine and James conferred in whispers from time to time, and Stephen tapped his pen against his teeth as he read, but Edith got straight down to the task. Annie smiled. She loved getting to know her students, and this exercise was very revealing.

As they wrote, there was the distant sound of a car followed by another. Annie looked at the door. Another couple in their fifties came in, followed by a breathless young woman with bright ginger hair, puffing her excuses for being late.

"You're fine," Annie said. "I've just asked everyone to fill in one of these forms, so we haven't quite started yet."

As Annie put on some music by Abba, the door opened for what turned out to be the last time that evening. Another young man came in by himself. "Is this the dancing class?"

"Yes, come on in. Lovely to meet you. I'm Annie, the teacher."

"My name's Mick. I haven't done any of this before."

"Don't think any of us have," Edith answered, before sticking her hand out for him to shake and introducing herself.

Mick looked nonplussed but returned her greeting before glancing around at the other people in the room. He gravitated towards the young woman, although he said nothing to her.

As the last few finished filling in their forms, Annie said, "Shall we get started? This music you will all know, I'm sure. It's a cha-cha-cha rhythm. I thought we'd start with something lively but not too difficult. Right, if all the men stand in a line on that side, and the ladies face them, I'll go through the men's steps first." She stood in front of the men's line, facing the same way as them. "Rock and replace, cha-cha-cha."

They were off.

She taught the women their mirroring steps. "Try to straighten each knee for the rock and replace. That gives a Cuban motion in the hips. Let's all try that again."

After several attempts, Annie turned and said, "Very good. Let's have a look at you. Don't forget to straighten those knees for the rock and replace. Wow, Stephen, very good. Straightening the knees helps with hip action."

There were some embarrassed reactions, but Edith gave him a clap.

"I'm going to put the music on, and we'll all try that, shall we?"

They made a passable attempt to keep in the rhythm as Annie called the steps.

"Now we need to take partners."

There was the old familiar shuffling Annie remembered from years ago. Some things never changed. The married couples went straight to it. Stephen held back and looked awkward. Mick made a beeline for the red-haired woman, who had introduced herself as Morag. "Shall we?"

"Mmm. Thanks, I'm normally the last to be picked for a team." Morag shrugged.

"Stephen, if you dance with Edith … but first come here, and I'll show you all the hold. You don't stand close in a Latin dance. More like this." Annie placed Stephen's hands and demonstrated to them all. He took it in good part, and Annie was aware of a collective 'phew' rippling across some members of the group at not having to be too intimate. She released Stephen and passed him across to Edith.

They all practised their rock, replace, cha-cha-cha while Annie called the moves out.

There was a good deal of laughter after the first few steps and a sharp intake of breath from Mick as Morag stepped on his toes.

"You don't need to stand too close together, Morag. Then that won't happen," Annie said.

"Sorry, I started to cha-cha-cha too early," she said, her vibrant curls bobbing as she tried again. "Now you know why I was always last to be chosen for a team. Such a lame brain."

"I think you're ready for music."

Abba's 'Gimme, Gimme, Gimme' sounded from the speaker. Annie showed them how to start by taking a sideways cha-cha-cha after the count of three before getting into the routine. When the music finished, there was a spontaneous round of applause before the group took sips from the water-bottles they had brought.

"It's quite energetic." Christine was puffing.

"It is if you haven't done any exercise for years," her husband said.

She looked sideways at him, drawing her lips together.

"That was really good," Edith said. "What a team."

"I thought we might learn a sequence dance now." Annie spoke into the mic. "It's quite an easy one and if you go to a social dance, chances are they'll do this one. It's quite common."

They all stood.

"You'll need a partner. It's called the Breakaway Blues. I'll show you. Mick, would you mind? Take my hands like this."

As Annie went through the steps with Mick, she was able to guide him in the right direction before she let him go. "There you are, and Morag's waiting for you." He headed back to Morag with alacrity, even though she'd stepped on his toes.

When the lesson finished, each member of the class came and thanked Annie and said how much they had enjoyed themselves.

"I've never done anything like this before," Morag said. "It was great exercise for the mind as well as the body. All that remembering what order things came in."

Mick dallied and seconded what she'd said.

"Same time next week, but I shall need to charge you full price from now on," said Annie. "Sorry. If it's not for you, and you want to pass on coming again, I quite understand."

"It's still good value, in my book," Christine said and glanced at her husband for confirmation.

"Oh yes," he said.

"Will you be back next week, Morag?" Mick asked.

"Yes, I think so."

"Thank you so much," Stephen said as the others left the room. "That was good fun."

Annie saw him wink at Edith as he left. She, in turn, came across and pumped Annie's hand.

"Just what the doctor ordered," she said. "Great fun, and good exercise too, for brain and body, as that other lass said."

"Yes, it is," Annie said and laughed with her as she packed away her music equipment.

CHAPTER 10

Harry stood in the doorway in silence and watched as Annie collected her things. All the students had left, and as she straightened her back, she stood for a moment, gazing across the gardens.

Outside was a wave of colour, and Harry remembered the shimmering scent of the blooms. They stirred his soul and made him wish his life had not been blighted by the pain he'd been responsible for all those years ago. The glare of the late afternoon sun had gone, and dusk began to settle. Lances of larkspur were punctuated by goldenrod, not yet in flower. Ruffles of velvet roses fluttered in the breeze.

Harry experienced an ache of longing as he looked at Annie again. Yet the secrets of his heart left him hollow. How could he think that he could ever take hold of her as her husband had once done? Whatever gave him the right to imagine that she might have affection for him? Anyway, he couldn't trust himself to get into a serious relationship. Not again.

He glanced down at his stomach and unconsciously sucked it in. His corduroy trousers were baggy, and his shoes were boats on his feet, one of which turned in a little. No matter how hard he tried, he would never be the neat, tidy sort who looked sleek and well-groomed. He was making a fool of himself. When his sister Lucy had been for a rare visit during the school holidays last year, she'd had a go at him about his condition, but it was daunting to lose weight, and why bother to smarten himself up? He had no one for whom to do that.

He'd cared for his wife, Sheila, and he had done his absolute best to ensure her happiness, but it hadn't been enough in the end. He had failed her when they'd needed each other the most, and he knew it. He'd been unable to be the support she craved because he was suffering as well. Always aware of the need to earn money to keep her and please her, he had spent too much time away, so that when the worst had happened, he had been completely preoccupied. Sheila couldn't forgive him any more than he could forgive himself. He knew now he had been running away. Eventually, she had left him for a younger man.

Annie turned and saw him. Her smile warmed his heart.

"How did it go? You seemed to have several here, judging by the number of cars in the yard."

"Oh, Harry, it was amazing!"

Her enthusiasm was infectious, and his own smile broadened.

"How many came?"

Annie listed the people. "I think they'll all come back next week. They said they would. You know, you should join in. I wouldn't charge you, of course."

"Oh no." Harry shrank inside, suddenly scared. "I would be hopeless. Look, two left feet these days, and not the right kind of rhythm in me anymore. It all left me several years ago." He indicated his turned-in foot.

"That's correctible to some extent. As for rhythm, I remember you on the disco floor, so don't give me that." She laughed. "What do you think of 'eMotion School of Dance' as a name? Is it catchy enough? It's a bit late now anyway. That's what it is on the social media sites. I hope it grabs people's attention. I'm sorry, I'm rabbiting on. Look, I'll leave you in peace." She continued to gather her things.

"It's catchy, modern and different. Would you like a cup of tea? The kettle's been on." Harry didn't want to sound like he was pleading, but he knew he might if he wasn't careful.

"I better get back. I want to make some notes about this evening. Thanks, though."

Deflated, he said, "I'll help you carry some of this to the car." He took hold of the speaker handle in one hand and her cloth bag in the other. Annie opened the door and stood back, then followed him out and along the path.

Harry smelled the roses. " You can't see so well in this light, but all those nasturtiums creeping along the ground and over the arch are amazing. All the shades of red and yellow and everything in between remind me of a painting."

"They bloom best in full sun, I think," Annie said.

Harry didn't know how to ask her for another meeting. Of course, he would see her this time next week when she came for her dance class, but he was disheartened at having to wait until then. He was in such turmoil. He shouldn't be going after her, not after what had happened in the past, but he couldn't help himself.

After Annie had left, he went in through the kitchen door and made himself a cup of tea. Sighing, he sat in the easy chair by the empty fireplace, put his cup on top of the coal scuttle and switched on the TV. As he flicked through the channels that did nothing to capture his attention, he sighed again.

Then he sat upright and turned off the set with determination. He stood and paced, before returning to his seat. Enough of this self-absorption. This attitude was no good at all, he thought, smacking his hands down onto his knees. He had come to a decision. Determined to take action, he hurried upstairs to his rooms.

CHAPTER 11

For the second week's lesson, Annie had two new couples, bringing the total to twelve people. They came in together, and it turned out they were friends who had egged each other on to come during a session at the pub.

I hope this is a serious move and not a light-hearted mistake, Annie thought. "It's half price for the first week," she said to the group. "Treat it as a taster to see if it's really for you. It's lovely to meet you. It should be fun, and it's good brain as well as body exercise," she added hopefully, remembering what Edith and Morag had said.

Annie had planned to repeat all the steps from the previous session to ensure everyone remembered what they had done, so the newcomers slotted in nicely.

Stephen nodded when Edith collared him to be her partner. "My pleasure. You're as light as a whisper in a dream." Stephen gave a small bow.

Edith simpered coyly and giggled.

Mick and Morag automatically gravitated towards each other. "You don't mind risking your toes again, then?" Morag laughed gently, and they smiled at each other.

Christine and James and all the other couples had arrived in their pairs, so that all worked neatly.

They moved on from a basic cha-cha-cha movement to include a New Yorker step. The only hiccup came when Christine moved in the wrong direction and her husband, James, pointed out her error. Despite his undertone, everyone was aware of the snipe. Mick and Morag exchanged glances and Stephen winked at Edith.

Annie walked them through the Breakaway Blues dance from the previous week, too. As they repeated it with some music, James got into a complete pickle. Christine forbore to state the obvious, but the job was done on her behalf, albeit in good humour, by both Mick and Stephen.

"Me and you are dancing like dogs," Stephen said to James. "Two left feet."

"Lost the plot, James?" Mick laughed and others joined in, but not unkindly.

James took the teasing from them in good part, although he gave Christine a scowl before turning his mouth to her ear. "It's because you were leading me instead of letting me take the lead," he muttered.

Again, this week there was much laughter, and everyone agreed the lesson had been fun.

"We're off to the pub in the village. Anyone fancy coming? It's a bit grungy in there, but it's handy." One of the new men addressed them all.

"Brilliant idea," Mick agreed. "Fancy a quick one, Morag?"

Morag looked flushed, but whether that was from the exercise or the invitation, Annie didn't know. She agreed, though.

Edith declined and so did Stephen, but James and Christine agreed to go. "I'm ready for a drink," she said. "It's thirsty work."

"It is that," James said and put his hand on Christine's back as they left the hall. "Are you coming, Annie?"

"Maybe another time. I've notes to write up and next week's lesson to plan, but thanks."

That bodes well, Annie thought. *If they socialise after the class, they're more likely to return, surely. Even James seemed more relaxed by the end.*

As they all left, Harry appeared. He enquired about what she had taught them but didn't offer her a cup of tea and stood at the door with keys in his hand.

"Glad it went well," he said. "See you soon. Must dash, things to do."

Stephen offered to carry Annie's equipment. As she followed the young man to their cars, she surprised herself by feeling disappointed at Harry's lack of pursuit. On the drive back home, she went over all that had happened both the previous week and this week. Perhaps he was offended that she had refused his offer of a cup of tea last week. She didn't want any romantic relationship, but she enjoyed his company as a friend. By the time she turned into her road, she'd decided to ask Ginny's opinion and went round straight away.

As they sat comfortably at the kitchen table, Ginny turned off the television in the corner and asked, "What's up?"

"How do you know anything's up?" Annie prevaricated.

"I've known you long enough, so come on, fess up. Is it the dance school? Oh, I hope not. Or is Si not playing ball?" After scrutinising Annie's face, she went on, "Ah, I bet I know." Gleefully, she put her chin down and looked at Annie from under raised brows. "It's Harry, isn't it?"

Annie hesitated.

"I knew it. C'mon. Tell all."

"Maybe." Annie shrugged. "I don't know, but let me tell you about the school first." She shared the evening's exploits with Ginny, sliding into safer territory.

"I can see it's going well. I'm so pleased for you, Annie."

"It's early days, of course, but it's a such relief. If my projections are accurate, the money will help, but it's great to see all these people learning a new skill and having a laugh while they do it. The room we're using is fantastic. There are so many possibilities. I could easily run a second class, or maybe one for children. We could even have a Saturday social dance or a Sunday afternoon tea dance."

"Wow! Slow down. No running before learning to walk," Ginny warned, and Annie laughed.

"No foxtrot before I cha-cha-cha."

"Now, tell me about Harry. No more sliding out of it."

Annie sat for a moment as she considered, taking a gulp of the fast-cooling tea. "I'm not sure, really. We were getting along quite well. Just as friends, I mean. That's all I want now."

"Are you sure?"

"Absolutely. I've got so much going on and anyway, no one could replace Rob."

"Of course not. Anyone else would be different. But that doesn't mean they'd be less to you, though."

Annie ignored that. "He seemed distracted. I hope I haven't upset him. He's a kind, thoughtful man, and I do owe him for setting me up with the ballroom."

"Have you done or said anything that could have hurt his feelings?"

"I don't think so. I mean, I refused a cup of tea last week, but that's all."

"Why was that? How did it come about?"

Annie explained why she'd wanted to get home. Her enthusiasm returned as she remembered the buzz she'd got from giving her first lesson, and her desire to get away and write it all down. She caught the look on Ginny's face. "What? What is it?" Annie asked.

"I can see how excited you are. Oh well, whatever it is with Harry, I'm sure it'll pass. You probably haven't time for anything else now, anyway. Roll on next week, then, and here's to continued success." She raised her cup at Annie before taking a slurp.

By the time Si called around several days later, Annie had updated her medium and long-term plans and forecasts. She'd added to her website and had penned a short article, which she planned to send to the local paper. She had no idea if they would want it, but there was an outside chance they might get in touch.

"Wow, sis, I'm impressed," Si said. "Who'd have thought, my sister the entrepreneur."

"I know. Back in the day, I'd never have been brave enough."

"Back in the day, you didn't need to even consider it. Rob provided for both of you."

"He did. Yes, he did." There was silence for a moment before she continued. "If things go on as they've started, I could run a second class and have classes for children. Who knows what else?"

"Don't go too fast, Annie. You need to consolidate first. I don't want to throw a dampener on it, but you've only been going for two weeks. You need to be sure this lot will keep coming."

"Yes, but if they don't, it might help to have a second string to my bow. I'd need help if I ran a children's class." She saw his expression. "I know, don't worry. I spend most of my days thinking about 'what ifs'. What if they don't turn up next week? What if David Troughton changes his mind? What if…" She grimaced. "I need to plan, but I won't get in too deep too quickly. I need to earn some money first."

Si had the good grace to come round the table and put his arms around her.

"Thank you, Si." It was so good to know that they were friends as well as siblings, and that she had his approval. "You could always take it up. It's a great hobby and a good way to meet people."

"I'll pass, thanks."

"Don't worry, I'm only teasing you." And she was, although it would have been fun to have him there. Her mind turned to young Stephen. Shame he didn't have a partner. She wasn't sure how long he would keep coming if he had to dance with Edith every week.

"I can see your mind is elsewhere again," Si said.

"Sorry, little bro? What was that?"

"I'm off. See you soon. Take care, and get some sleep."

CHAPTER 12

Harry's plan had started to take shape. He spoke with a degree of cunning as well as genuine interest at the end of Annie's second class and learned what she had been teaching. He didn't have time to offer her a cup of tea, so eager was he to get back to his room, write down what she had said and find his iPad. A new vibrancy jittered through him after years of lethargy.

Back in his rooms, he typed 'Breakaway Blues' into the search bar and was happy to find that the first result was a video clip with a walkthrough of the routine. Perfect. The next in the list was the same thing with accompanying music. It was a gentle lilting rhythm, not too speedy, and the man and woman in the clip made it look easy. A further short film had the same thing but in a different rhythm. He decided to stick with the first one. In his head, he heard Annie calling the steps in her soft and gentle way. He'd been in the large square hall, straining to listen through the closed door. He wasn't going to admit to Annie what he was planning until he had made a good start by himself. He sensed he needed to spring a surprise if he were to grab her interest.

Next, he looked up the basic cha-cha-cha step and found a confident American dancing with a young woman in a red dress. There were clear instructions. After bookmarking the page, he couldn't resist having a go.

He propped the iPad on the chest of drawers in his room. It was hard to remember to straighten his knees and get his hips going. Then he caught sight of himself in the long mirror. Oh Lord. Who was he kidding? He put his hands to either side of his head as he looked at himself, and the voice on the iPad carried on. His feet were like slabs of meat in his outdoor shoes. His stomach hung over his trousers and as he turned, he caught sight of how baggy they were around his backside. His shirt was crumpled. He was a sorry sight. How could anyone look at him with anything but pity or plain old friendship? Even that was unlikely. Annie must have been being kind because that was who she was.

He sat on the end of the bed and reviewed his plan with despondency. For several moments, he was inclined to give up before he'd started.

Then he pulled his shoulders down, straightening his back. He'd made a resolution, and it was stupid to be so defeatist. He retrieved his iPad and turned to sit in his chair by the window. Looking out across the grass to the trees beyond, he was lost in thought.

The second part of his plan also required the internet. He looked up Slimming World and Weightwatchers. They both involved meetings, but he didn't want to confess to anyone what he was doing. There would be too many people to explain himself to, and he didn't have the confidence for that. He might see someone he knew, and word could get back to Annie. He would be a laughing stock. No, that wasn't fair. She wouldn't mock him. She was far too kind. He wanted his achievement to be a surprise, though.

This time, following more research, he bought and downloaded a book. The 5-2 diet would be hard. He'd have to plan meals; think ahead to ensure he had the right stuff in the fridge. He could start walking a bit further, too. Wasn't it supposed to be a combination of diet and exercise that made a difference? He'd have to speak to Mrs M and tell her he was going to prepare his own meals from now on. Maybe he'd tell her it was doctors' orders.

As he contemplated, he realised he hadn't been to the pub since that embarrassing incident when he'd bought the drinks and been abandoned. He didn't want to bump into any of those guys, but he realised he hadn't had the urge to drink much either. Maybe he'd start looking for extra jobs he could do in this great mausoleum. He'd better speak to David. There could be money involved in that.

This was going to be one hell of a challenge, but he had more determination than ever before.

"David, I do think we should tackle these leaks and stains on the ceilings. It'll only get worse next winter, and then it'll cost a whole lot more."

David shook his head and sucked air in through his teeth. "I suppose so… I don't know. I'll think about it."

"You know, I do believe you said that after last winter, but time is running out." Harry stood with his hands on his hips.

"You're right." David sighed. "It just seems such a huge job. I don't know where to start."

"Let's get a couple of companies out to give us estimates. If they give us separate ones for each area, we can decide what to do first. It's the sections of the roof we need done. I can do the internal stuff. There's the ballroom roof too. That's the worst place for the leaks. I'm seriously worried the whole ceiling could come down. That could be a catastrophe."

"For that friend of yours, you mean?" David gusted another sigh. "Alright. Get someone to look at the main roof first. We can look at the ballroom roof next time. You sorted those slipped tiles. It'll keep for a while now."

Harry had the upper hand now. "They could take a quick look at the ballroom. We don't have to take them up on it. If we just get a quote…"

"Oh, very well, but we'll see about the main roof first," David said. "That'll be more than enough for now." He picked up his newspaper, and Harry understood this was as far as he was going to get this time. It was a major step forward, though.

The next morning, Harry was awake at first light. He leapt out of bed, determined to find some companies who would come and give quotes before David had a chance to prevaricate some more. There were other jobs he would crack too, and he needed to go shopping to get some fat-free food. Later, he'd have a walk through the dances that Annie was teaching.

He realised he was smiling at nothing as he made himself a cup of tea. For such a long time, happiness had been shambling away from him. Now slivers of sunlight shot through the gloom reminding Harry of that time in school when they were told of Oscar Wilde and why he hadn't 'turned over a new leaf' while in Reading Gaol. The author's response had been that he hadn't yet reached the bottom of that page. The imagery had made Harry smile at the time. He pictured Annie as she had sat in a shaft of sunlight under the classroom window with dust motes dancing around her shining hair. *It was probably chalk dust*, he thought prosaically as he remembered. Well, now, he had reached the end of his page.

He would bury the awful past, ready to move forward.

But was Annie ready? That was the big question.

CHAPTER 13

Annie's phone rang at the crack of dawn. She snatched it up, still half asleep.

"I'm really sorry," said the voice at the other end. "We shan't be coming tonight."

"Who is it, please?" she asked.

"Sorry. It's Christine, from dancing. You know?"

"Oh yes. Yes, of course."

Annie sat up. She closed her eyes, although she was fully awake by this time. This was it. The first of several, perhaps. She hadn't managed to hit the right note. Perhaps the lesson was too easy and dull, or perhaps too difficult. She was so sure they had enjoyed it. They'd all said they'd be back. Easy to say when face to face, though. Still, Christine had the guts to call her. She could have emailed. That would have been the easy option. Annie was not surprised it was her. She suspected James was a domineering man but when it came to the difficult things, he didn't have the spine to deal with them. Annie imagined him in the background, dictating what his wife should do and say.

Christine continued. "It's James, you see."

Mmm, I can imagine, Annie thought.

"He's lost his voice and has a temperature."

"I'm sorry to hear that," she said, in her best calm voice.

"Sorry to bother you so early. I have a request. We're both so disappointed, you see. You will keep our places open, won't you? Please?" Annie could hear anxiety in Christine's voice.

"Well, yes, absolutely." She straightened her back.

"Oh good, that's a relief. I was worried. I said to James, I better phone right away."

Annie smiled, her tension released. She was utterly relieved. "Please don't fret. I look forward to seeing you both next week. I do hope James gets better quickly and you don't succumb."

"There's just one other thing."

"Yes?"

"We have four friends. They'd like to come along. We were telling them what fun it is and how it's good exercise too. Would you have space for them? I know they've missed a couple of weeks but, well, I do hope it would be alright. I think James would enjoy it even more if there were others coming who we know."

Annie's smile became a grin. She was tempted to bounce up and down on the mattress. "That would be lovely," she said with as much restraint as she could summon. "What are their names? I'll watch out for them. Do they know where to come and what time?"

"Yes, I'll make sure of all that, and again I'm so sorry about James."

"Don't worry. Of course, if you want to come on your own, I'm sure I could partner you for most of the lesson."

"Oh, I don't know. I'm not really used to going out on my own in the evenings. Perhaps I will, though. I'll talk to James about it."

"Yes, right. Well, I'll look forward to meeting your friends and if you come too that would be great."

They said their goodbyes and Annie cut the call. She sat for several moments in a mix of relief and euphoria. At this rate she'd need an assistant.

The doors were unlocked when Annie arrived for the class that evening but there was no sign of Harry. She was eager to get set up so assumed she would see him at the end of her session.

There was a little worm of disquiet somewhere inside her. She didn't want to think she'd hurt his feelings in any way. He was such a kind, gentle man, clearly lacking confidence. Annie hoped her using the ballroom, albeit for a pittance, would help him to see his home and job as more secure. They'd all be in the muck if David gave up. Maybe she needed a cunning plan in that direction.

Her thoughts were interrupted as Christine arrived with one of the new couples.

"How lovely to see you," Annie said. "I'm so pleased you came. It's not always easy, is it?"

"I'm not used to coming out at night without James. It seems all wrong."

"I completely understand that." Annie placed her hand on Christine's arm. "Believe me, it gets easier, and he'll be with you next week, I'm sure."

"Yes, he's starting to feel a little better."

For the first half of the lesson Annie repeated the things they had learned previously. Stephen moved nearer Christine as they started, but accepted Edith for his partner when she advanced towards him with purpose. Annie could see that she glowed at the prospect. Her lined face split into a beaming smile, her eyes twinkled, and a flush rose up her neck and across her cheeks. The new couples joined in and picked up what they had missed. Annie moved the class on and started to teach a basic waltz step.

"This is a basic progressive move. Some people will teach a box step first, which is fine, but with that you would stay in one place on the dancefloor. It's useful if you want to avoid someone else if the floor's busy, but with a progressive step you can move around straight away."

She showed the men and then the women when to use heels and when to rise on to their toes, and she counted the familiar one, two, three rhythm while they practised.

"Stephen, can I use you to show the hold?"

Having been paired, they all had a go and managed to move across the floor in a straight line.

"Try and keep it as smooth as possible. That's good. Let's have a go with some music."

At the end of the lesson, Christine agreed to accompany her friends to the pub for a drink. Annie smiled at her with encouragement. Mick and Morag left together, though they had indicated they wouldn't be at the local pub. Annie wondered whether they planned to go on somewhere, too.

"Thank you, Stephen," Edith said. "You're going to be a lovely dancer. So light on your feet."

He glanced at Annie before saying, "No worries. See you next week."

"Yes, oh yes, I hope so." Edith fluttered and faffed as she collected her things. "Goodnight." She smiled at Stephen as she left.

"If it's a problem, you having to dance with Edith every week, I can move things around a bit, I'm sure," Annie said as she walked him to the door.

"No, not really. She has good rhythm. I was hoping my ex-girlfriend might change her mind, so we could make up and she could come with me, but that's not to be."

"Oh dear. Had you been together long?"

"About six months. Not so long, I suppose. I should have seen the signs. They'd been there for weeks. Never mind, easy come…" Stephen shrugged. "Edith's a lovely old soul. It's fine."

There was no sign of Harry as Annie packed away her things, preparing to make the second trip to her car. Now the lesson was over, the worm of worry was wriggling again. She couldn't decide whether to stick her head into the hall and call out, but she didn't want to disturb David or intrude on their space. She was still on probation here. It could all turn sour so easily. As she stood, undecided and anxious, the inner door opened and Harry came in. Did he look a bit different? No, probably not.

"Hi," he said and smiled.

Perhaps everything was alright after all. *I've been panicking and worrying about nothing*, Annie thought.

"Good session?"

"Yes, I think so," she said. "I had two more new couples. I shall need an assistant at this rate. Someone young who doesn't want much pay." She grimaced.

"Try an ad at the library or the college. There may be a student who learned somewhere."

"There were others at Just Dance before it closed, too. How are you? I haven't seen you properly for a while."

"Oh, busy, busy."

"Maybe we could go for a walk again or grab a coffee?" She laughed, her nerves jangling.

"Yes, we should do that." He didn't offer a day, though.

Annie backed off. "I better get going. Thanks, Harry."

"What for?"

"Arranging this place. Giving me sensible advice. You're a good friend, and I'm pleased I bumped into you. Literally." She laughed again.

He looked wistful, she thought. She was puzzled about his reticence, yet he seemed friendly enough again.

"Right, goodnight," he said, as if dismissing her.

"See you soon," Annie said as she turned to go. Heading to her car, she was surprised to realise her heart was heavy.

As Harry watched Annie leave, it was all he could do not to run after her and tell her how much he loved her. He loved her courage. He loved her tenacity when faced with obstacles. And he loved her hair, her eyes, her hips as they swayed down the path. If only she saw him as more than a friend. But she didn't know what he had done in the past, and if she did that would put an end to their friendship anyway.

Okay. He would be companionable, affable, helpful. Already he was working on his health. As he'd stood listening at the door, he'd desperately wanted to be in there learning with the others, with Annie. He would do it, though. He would surprise her one day.

As he moved back and forth across the hall with his broom when everyone had gone, he did so in a waltz step. One two three, one two three. Heel, toes, toes, heel, toes, toes.

There was normally a click as the door opened, but Harry must not have heard it. The next thing he knew, David was leaning against the jamb with his arms folded, regarding him. As Harry turned for his next sweep, he realised he had been caught red-handed, looking like an idiot.

"Just getting in a bit of practice, are we?" David said.

Harry sniggered, completely at a loss for what to say.

"I used to dance quite a bit, a long time ago. It's a bit like the proverbial bicycle-riding, though," David said as he advanced into the room.

"I could do with your help, then," Harry said. "Instead of standing there, you could give me some tips."

"You are looking a bit robotic and wooden. The waltz must flow. You need to feel the music and sway a little with it. And step out. Don't be inhibited."

"You wouldn't care to demonstrate, would you?"

"You must be joking."

"Honestly, David, I'm serious." Harry rested on his broom handle.

With a sigh, David lifted his eyes to the ceiling, but still he raised his arms as if holding a partner. Then, as weightless as a shadow, he glided around the floor. "Well, come on, then. I'm not acting like a lemon for you to stand and watch. Follow my actions, man."

To begin with, it was like a parody. The tall, skeletal man and the shorter, rotund one echoing his moves might have been laughable, if they had not been so serious in their endeavours. Both lost in the moment, for different reasons, they swayed and revolved, Harry unconsciously mimicking the reverses and natural turns that David was demonstrating as well as the basic progressive step that he had been teaching himself.

All too soon, David stopped. "Right, that's enough fooling for one night. I'll leave you to it." He left abruptly without saying why he had shown his face in the first place.

Harry, puffing a little, watched the door close before taking hold of his broom and waltzing around one more time, displaying more confidence with each step.

Weight has nothing to do with it, he thought. *I can be light on my feet despite my shape.* He thought better of himself than he had done for an exceedingly long time. All he had to do now was hope Annie noticed him in a different way. He wished her well with her enterprise, he truly did, and he longed to support and cherish her. If only Rob hadn't been such perfection. He was up against it.

CHAPTER 14

Annie was lonely. She needed to share her success and while Si was proud of her, he looked at her new venture with a business mind. She wanted to be loved for her personal successes, as well as the things she was achieving financially and physically. It was the minutiae of life, too, that she wanted to share with someone. When she awoke in the morning and the sun blasted through her curtains, she wanted to tell someone of the joy she was beginning to experience again after all this time. When it rained, she needed to sit quietly with another person, not speaking but relishing each other's company. She had conquered the three peaks of anger, guilt, and depression. Now she needed to conquer the great mountain of loneliness.

Rob didn't want me to be like this.

Annie did what she always did when she was low. She went down the road to see Ginny. As she walked in the early morning freshness, she felt suddenly guilty. It was unfair to use Ginny in this way. As soon as her friend opened the door, Annie said, "Sorry, it's me again. I need company. Are you in for a cuppa?"

"Don't be silly." Ginny held the door wide. "And stop that 'sorry' nonsense. It goes both ways. Surely you know that by now. What about the time Ellie had that roaring temperature, and remember when I was in hospital with my appendix? Who stepped in without question? We're friends, Annie. It's what we do." Moving to the bottom of the stairs, she called up, "Ellie? Annie's here. Do you want tea or are you off out?"

"Coming!" A muffled reply sounded from upstairs, then Ellie came bounding into the kitchen. "Hi, Annie." She gave Annie a hug. "How ya doing?"

"Fine, and you?"

"I'm good, thanks. Jack an' I are going roller-skating later, so I can't stop long. Been preening. Gotta fly. Y'know how it is."

"Not sure I do, these days. Still going strong, then, you and Jack?"

"Yeah. We're a couple now."

"Right." Annie glanced at Ginny, who gave her a subtle wink. "What were you before, then?"

"Oh, you know. Just seeing each other."

"Right…" Annie said. "Okay. Well … good, then." She caught Ginny's eye again, and her friend gave a slight shrug. "The vocab of this generation is in another world now."

"You could try again, Annie. You should try Partner.com — you know, the dating site. I know it's all a new idea," Ellie said, "but that's where we met. It's all good, you know. Like, safe and everything."

"Ellie!" Ginny sounded mortified.

"Mmm." Annie was non-committal. She turned to Ginny and shook her head gently. "It's okay."

"We all do it," Ellie continued. "It's the way to go, these days. Gotta keep up, Annie."

Annie laughed. "I know, but it doesn't get any easier."

"Okay, I'm off." Ellie kissed her mother. "Jack will be waiting."

"Can't keep Jack waiting," Ginny said. "Go on with you. And take this hairspray and brush before you go."

"I'll do it when I come back. Gotta fly. Bye. Love you." The front door banged shut.

"God, she's like a tornado," Ginny puffed.

"And who does she get that from?" Annie smiled.

Annie was drifting as she finished the ironing. In her mind, she was back in the ballroom, sharing her expertise with the beginners: the waltz, the cha-cha-cha, the sequence dance she had taught. Images of her pupils and their quirky styles came to her. Many were stepping mechanically, and their lips moved as they silently counted. There were stilted steps without sway but faces full of concentration. It was all very normal, and she would enjoy seeing them progress as time went by.

Thoughts swirled. She had seen development in them already, and not just with their dancing. Christine had arrived without James when he was poorly, and she knew from personal experience that could be a challenge. Mick was forming a friendship with Morag, and even she had gained confidence. Hopefully, that would continue, and she'd be less clumsy. Then images of Harry shot into her head, and she wondered why he had been so distant. She hadn't even seen him the last two weeks she was there. She had told him she only wanted to be friends, so perhaps he had found someone else in whom to take an interest. She switched off the iron and plonked down onto the edge of the spare bed behind her. Again, she thought, *I'm lonely. I want to share my success with someone.*

Then the realisation struck like a thunderbolt. She was ready to move on. She *needed* companionship, and yes … love. She wanted someone's arms around her and to rest her head in the crook of someone's shoulder. She would soon be forty years old. The future stretched ahead, long, empty, and forlorn. She was solitary and hollow like a void with no prospect of sharing what should be exhilarating. It was becoming a physical pain.

Where to meet people? All her old friends were attached. That had been the reason why she had turned down so many kind invitations. They were all so happy and fulfilled, which had emphasised her loneliness.

Perhaps she should try the Partner thing, like Ellie suggested. That was scary, though. Maybe she'd just Google it to get the gist.

She leapt up and ran downstairs. "Right, let's put the kettle on," she said to Raffa.

With her cup of tea next to her elbow, she sat at the table in the kitchen, turned on her laptop and typed 'Partner' into Google. She then spent the next half an hour watching video clips and reading about the best way to proceed. It became more and more disorientating, the more she read. The content of her biography, the opening gambit, things to avoid, and ways of introducing herself that were not too cheesy were all up for consideration. Maybe she was going about it the wrong way. She was being too analytical. Honesty was always the best policy. She wasn't desperate, so what did it matter if nothing came of it?

Annie got onto Partner.com and found the form to fill in. She attached some presentable photographs and then composed a few facts about herself, the area in which she lived, and then her interests. When she'd finished, she couldn't resist looking at other people's profiles.

"Ah, Raffa, look at him," she said when she found someone who struck her fancy. "Should I indicate I like the look of him?"

The man had a nice smile with kind eyes and the right amount of grey at his ears. He liked going to the cinema and dancing. Annie took a deep breath and indicated that she would like to meet him. Now all she had to do was wait.

Perhaps there'd be a few more to tick. She looked again. There was no point putting all her eggs in one basket, so to speak. As she scanned profiles, there were a couple more that seemed alright.

Goodness knows what Harry would say if he knew I was doing this, she thought. *But clearly he's moving on too. Good for us! We both need to get on with life.*

CHAPTER 15

Harry had kept out of Annie's way for the last few weeks, all the better to surprise her. He was doing well with both his health and his dancing ability. The DVD he had bought was a great help, and he was pleased to realise that his confidence was returning.

Tonight, he decided, would be the night to see Annie again. He was excited. He dressed in trousers that had hung in his wardrobe for many years, which now fitted again. They were fresh from the dry-cleaner and the style was traditional, so they hadn't gone out of fashion. He had a shirt, the colour of which complemented his blue eyes, and he shaved with care, splashing on some expensive cologne that he saved for special occasions. He looked at himself in the long mirror in his rooms. A few weeks of being strict about his diet had been hard. There was temptation when he was sitting alone in the evenings. Several times he had fought his desire to nip out to the pub or the local shop to buy a beer or some snack that would have broken his regime. He had managed thus far to keep himself in check. Now, as he regarded his returning waistline, he congratulated himself. He ought to consider buying a newer pair of trousers, but he'd hold off until he'd lost a little more weight.

He waited for the end of Annie's dance lesson with breathless anticipation, the like of which he couldn't remember ever experiencing before.

He started listening at the door for the gist of tonight's exercises so that he could continue practising, but he was distracted and couldn't concentrate.

After an age, he heard Annie say goodnight to her students and then the sound of the outside door opening and closing. He took a deep breath and entered the ballroom.

Almost all the class had left. Just one man was still there. Annie was still packing her bag as Harry approached her. The enormous space between them made him nervous, and when he said her name it came out too loud, making her jump.

"Harry, you startled me. How are you? I haven't seen you for a while."

"I've been busy. This and that." He glanced at the man. When he'd watched the students leaving over the last few weeks, he hadn't seen him among them.

"Harry, this is Nigel. He's come to meet me. We're going for a drink together at a new place on the edge of town."

Harry wished the ground would open so he could disappear. He was short of breath, and his heart began to jump. He nodded at Annie's date. It was as much as he could manage.

"Yes, the Rosé Glow? Do you know it? Perhaps not your scene," Nigel said.

Was he looking Harry up and down?

"I wasn't sure where it is, so Nigel kindly said he'd come to meet me so I could follow him." A small frown puckered Annie's forehead.

Was she scrutinising Harry more closely than usual? Perhaps that was wishful thinking.

"Shall I carry the speaker to your car?" Nigel asked Annie. "Don't want you straining those pretty arms."

She turned to him and smiled. "Thank you," she said as she handed him her car key.

He seemed a little patronising, Harry thought. He's standing there in his pale trousers looking over-styled, over-rated, over smooth. Taking Annie for a drink. His Annie.

After Nigel had left the room, Harry asked, "Where did you meet him?" He tried to sound unconcerned but was aware that his voice sounded staccato — accusing, even.

"If I tell you, you mustn't laugh."

"Of course not."

"It was on Partner.com."

Harry's head shot back and his eyes opened wide. "Oh, wow. Er ... I see."

"I'm told everyone's doing it now, and it's quite safe. We'll go in our own cars to the bar and leave that way too. We've texted quite a bit. It's not like a blind date. Better than that because we already know, from the process we had to follow, that we have some shared interests."

"Annie, you don't need to justify it to me," Harry said as gently as he could, while he seethed inside with frustration.

Nigel returned. Nodding at Harry, he took Annie's bag in one hand and her elbow in the other in a proprietorial way. "Ready?" He steered her towards the door.

Annie, in a thoughtful mood, followed Nigel to the Rosé Glow. Harry looked different, but she couldn't quite put her finger on it. He was certainly smarter and he smelled lovely. Sort of lemony and heady. He must have been moving on, too. Perhaps some woman had had a hand in his new look. Wasn't that usually the reason for somebody losing weight and smartening themselves up? Annie wasn't sure how she felt about that. Still, she was trying to move on, so perhaps she should be pleased for him.

As she pulled up outside the bar, Nigel appeared at her car door and opened it with a flourish. Annie smiled up into his handsome, sparkling eyes. He extended his hand and helped her out. It was a long time since she had experienced anything so gallant. Rob and she had been too comfortable with each other for such theatricals, but she appreciated that this good-looking man was trying to seem suave for her benefit.

She looked up at the pink neon name of the wine bar. It looked sophisticated and elegant. She hoped she would do it, and her companion, justice. Her outfit had been chosen with care. It had to be suitable for teaching her students and for this outing, so she wore a peacock-blue dress and she had exchanged her thin black cardigan for a pashmina. In the car, she had added a pair of blue drop earrings and touched up her lipstick. Her black, heeled shoes clattered as she crossed the pavement, passed through the door that Nigel held open for her, and stepped across the Italian tiled floor.

Nigel guided her to a tall stool next to a small, round table. She managed to clamber on without looking too ungainly. Whoever had thought this trendy seating was attractive to women needed to think again. Seated on high, Annie was aware of needing to keep her knees together. It wasn't comfortable.

"Shall we share a bottle?" Nigel asked.

"I think a glass would be fine. White, please. Perhaps a Pinot Grigio or a Sauvignon." As he beckoned for a waiter, Annie took a swift look around. In the main, the clientele was young and vibrant. She was a little out of place. *Oh, well, live dangerously*, she thought, trying to give herself courage.

An enormous glass of wine arrived, and Nigel sat opposite her with his glass of red. He made a great play of taking in the aroma, looking at it against the light and swirling it around the glass before taking a sip. Then he appeared to swish it around his mouth before swallowing. Annie took a gulp of hers, unsure whether he was nervous or arrogant. He was good-looking, though, and underneath all her anxiety and uncertainty she was flattered that he had chosen her. She watched his Adam's apple move up and down as he swallowed, and she experienced a small thrill somewhere deep inside.

As the hour passed, they both loosened up. Annie was driving, so she declined another glass. She remembered that Nigel had said he liked dancing on his Partner profile, so she asked him about that.

He gave her a sheepish look. "Mmm, not quite honest there."

"Oh?"

"No one tells the whole truth on those things, do they? I have done a small amount of rock and roll, and that was a long time ago, but hey, who's checking?"

I told the truth. The thought flitted through Annie's mind, but very soon they were chatting easily about other things.

By the time they said goodbye, it was late. The wine had worn off with the tiny but strong espresso coffee that followed, and Annie was tired but happy and relaxed. When Nigel asked her for a second date, she agreed.

He took her keys from her hand and with a sweep, he opened her car door before handing them back to her. Before she had time to wonder what she thought of this, he grabbed her hand kissed the back of it, then looked into her eyes and winked.

"Until next Saturday, then," he said, and twinkled a smile.

CHAPTER 16

When Annie arrived for the next lesson with her little group, there were two other couples waiting in the parking area.

This could be tricky, she thought. *I've been going for too many weeks now for new beginners to catch up, and I haven't got capacity for more when I'm on my own anyway. I don't want to turn anyone away, though.* Thinking on her feet, Annie knew she could start another beginners' class after this one in four weeks' time.

"Hello. Do come along to the hall," she invited the newcomers before marching along the path. One of the men opened the door for her.

When she switched on the lights, there was a gasp and the women in the little group exclaimed as they looked around at the Georgian splendour and the fine proportions of the room.

"This is unexpected," said a tiny-framed lady.

"It's perfect. Look at this floor!" said the other.

The man who had held the door said, "This will do very nicely. Plenty of space for stepping out, especially for the foxtrot."

The fourth was still looking around with a broad smile lightening his heavy features.

"How can I help you?" Annie asked, looking from one to the other. They spoke as if they had experience. The foxtrot was not a dance for complete beginners.

The man who had held the door introduced himself. "My name's Ted Brown. This is my wife, Judy." The small lady held out her hand and Annie shook it. "This is Cameron McKay and his wife Gillian," Ted continued.

There was more nodding and handshaking.

"We used to dance, and we've all got our silver Latin. We did rumba, tango, and cha-cha-cha. For rock and roll we did gold, but that was a long time ago. With ballroom we have silver for waltz, quickstep, and then bronze for foxtrot, except for Gill. She's the expert."

"And I'm very happy for a refresher," Gill interrupted with a knowing smile.

"How long ago are we talking?" Annie asked.

"A good three years," Ted said.

"More like four or five," Cameron interjected. "We're all older than we thought!"

"Speak for yourself," Gillian said and nudged him in the ribs with her elbow.

"The thing is," Ted went on, "Judy and I have just moved here and reconnected with our friends. What we're looking for is someone to help us go over what we learned before and maybe even take us on further." He looked at his companions for agreement. "Your website said you were qualified for that. Gill could do some of it, but she's decided she's not up to teaching us if she's doing it by herself."

"Yes, I'm qualified," Annie said. "I've got my International Dance Teachers' Association certificates and I have a Fellowship, too. I'm mainly ballroom, Latin and classical sequence — oh, and rock and roll — but I have done some training for street dance, line dance, and cheerleading."

Ted laughed again, as did the others. They were a jolly quartet. "Oh, I don't think we're into street dance," he said.

Annie was excited. She got a genuine thrill from the progress of the beginners, but this was a challenge of a different kind and would do her reputation no end of good. "If I'm to give you lessons, the only evening I have available would be this one each week, after the class of beginners I'm about to teach. Ah, here come some of them."

The door opened and Stephen came in, followed by Mick and Morag.

Annie had leaflets in her bag with her qualifications, hourly rate, contact details, and photographs of the premises. She'd designed them and had them printed by a local company. "Perhaps you'd like to take these and call me." Then she had a hasty rethink and changed tack. You weren't supposed to let people escape that easily. "On the other hand, you could book a taster session now, for next week, and we'll take it from there. It's half price for the first week." While they looked at each other, she fished her diary out.

Ted spoke up for the four of them. "Well, yes. That'd be splendid. Thank you. Next week it is, then. Half price, you say?"

"For the first lesson, yes." Annie confirmed the time and grinned.

"Aye, that'd be grand," he said. "See yer next week then, lass."

Annie was still grinning like a mad thing as she taught her beginners the next steps in the waltz. "Okay, gentlemen. You will be turning to your left and leading your lady. So, turning left is your left foot forwards. Maintain side and close before your right foot goes backwards, and again side and close. Like this." She demonstrated the men's footwork. "Ladies, you will mirror that. When his left foot goes forwards, your right foot will go back."

She got all the men to practise and copy behind her before asking the ladies to do their steps.

"Gentlemen, this is a left turn for you, or more accurately a reverse turn. Now, you need to ensure you step between your lady's feet, not outside. Christine, may I borrow you for a moment? I'll take the man's steps. Like this." Annie managed to steer her partner while demonstrating the steps for the men.

After several goes, Morag trod on Mick's foot and sent him hopping, which put a temporary halt on the proceedings while she apologised profusely. He tried to maintain some composure while reassuring her, through a fixed grin, that he was fine.

"You need to ensure you step between your partners feet, gentlemen. Ladies, don't try and step out of the way because that's when you risk being trodden on," Annie said.

"I think I put my foot in the wrong place." Mick spoke to Morag. "It was my own fault, not yours."

Morag looked up at her partner and smiled with gratitude. Annie experienced a little flutter of pleasure on their behalf.

"Moving on, if we only do that," Annie said, "we'll be going around in circles, getting dizzy and not progressing around the room at all. We need to learn a natural turn as well. It's basically the same in reverse." She proceeded to show them, placing her right foot forward this time and encouraging the men to have a go while keeping the one, two, three rhythm.

"This is magic," Christine said. "I know we're all a bit wooden at the moment, but I can see why it became the dance of romance."

"It's good," said James. "Like real professionals doing proper dancing. Vienna and all that." He smiled at her.

"Next week, I'm going to begin another sequence which is immensely popular, and most social dances you might go to will do it at some point. We'll be doing the first eight bars of the Sweetheart Waltz."

Annie was on cloud nine. By the end of the lesson, when Stephen came to thank her, she was buzzing with enthusiasm.

"It's a pleasure. Are you enjoying it?"

"I am." He hesitated.

"Is there a problem?"

"Not a problem as such." Again, he didn't speak immediately.

"Go on. Anything you say will be between us alone."

"It's Edith. This is awkward and makes me sound arrogant."

Annie waited while he composed what he needed to say. Then she spoke quietly. "I know you well enough now to know you aren't."

"It's just ... I think she sees me as different to say ... a son." He coloured. "I think she has a bit of a crush. I know that sounds stupid. I'm less than half her age."

"What leads you to think this, Stephen? If you're uncomfortable I can arrange something else, I'm sure."

"No, no. It's my overactive imagination. Please forget I said anything. Truly. I'm good. I must be off. Thanks, again."

With that he turned and scurried away, leaving Annie wondering. She would need to keep an eye on things. She hadn't noticed anything, but if he was getting uncomfortable, she didn't want to lose him. She hadn't bargained for such an event.

Just then the internal door opened, and Harry approached. "Hi."

"Hello, Harry." Annie turned to him with a smile. He did look different, but she still couldn't quite say how. His clothes fitted better, for sure. She breathed in his aftershave, that same heady but delicate scent. "How are you?"

"I'm fine, thanks. How did your lesson go?"

"It was good. Things do seem to be taking off." Why she was suddenly stilted with him, she didn't know. He was skirting around her too, as if he wasn't coming to the real point.

"I've got some more clients wanting intermediate lessons. Not beginners. Do you think I could have the hall for an extra hour? It would be the same evening. After this class, like now, starting next week."

"I can check with David. I'm sure it won't be a problem."

"Thanks." Annie breathed a sigh of relief. Still he hovered, so Annie turned to pack up her music.

"How did your date go?"

Ah, was this the real purpose of him lingering?

"It was fine. We chatted easily after the first few minutes. He seemed very charming, opening the car door and so on."

"I see." Then he mumbled, "Sounds a right gigolo."

Annie glanced back at him, but he looked away. She was puzzled. He sounded irritable and unlike his usual self.

"Seeing him again, then?"

"Yes. For dinner on Saturday."

"Have a nice time." He turned away and muttered something.

"Sorry?"

"Nothing. Must get on."

As he left, Annie could have sworn he mumbled something about a walk seeming tame. As for that word 'gigolo'! That sounded ridiculous. Was he cross?

CHAPTER 17

Harry couldn't get the image of Annie's smooth-looking date out of his head. Good Lord, had he really used the word 'gigolo'? *What an idiot I must have sounded*, he thought. *How can I compete with Nigel? I don't have the money to take her to flash restaurants. How can going for a walk across the meadows with the dog match up to what he's offering?*

The next time Annie arrived for her class, Harry couldn't resist asking how her date had gone. It was like worrying at a wound.

"How was your weekend?"

"It was okay," she replied, bending over her bag to unpack her sound system.

"Did you have a good meal?"

"The food was lovely. It's such a posh place that if the meal was scorched or raw it wouldn't have taken the shine off the service and the surroundings, but it wasn't. It was all delicious."

Annie seemed to be deliberately not sharing what Harry needed to know. She had said nothing about the company. Had the guy held her hand? Had he touched her hair? Had he kissed her when he saw her home? The questions were coming faster and were more frantic. Should he ask her? There was no way he could do that casually.

Harry realised that several awkward, silent moments had passed. He'd have to go. She'd think he was being creepy, hanging around like this. He sighed. "See you later," he muttered.

Stephen was the first to arrive for the next class. Annie noticed he had new dancing shoes. "Nice," she said, nodding at them.

"If I'm going to keep coming, I might as well have the proper gear."

"Listen, if it's a problem dancing with Edith, I'm sure I can sort something else out." She wasn't sure what, truth be told.

"No, it's fine, really. I want to learn to dance." Stephen chuckled and shrugged. "That might even help me with the ladies. You never know."

Annie decided to keep an eye on things, though. She didn't want to risk losing either of them. It was too soon for students to drop off.

The door opened and several of the others arrived. When Edith came, Annie noted she went to sit next to Stephen. He looked up at her and smiled as she greeted him. Annie turned to her music. Nothing to worry about, surely.

Then her heart swooped as the door from the house opened. It was none other than David Troughton. He carried a lightweight wooden chair with a raffia seat, which he placed against the wall next to the door and sat on, with legs crossed and arms folded. Annie made a move towards him, but he raised the flat of his hand to indicate she didn't need to. She decided to get on with her lesson, but her heart was thumping so hard she was sure someone would see it. It was worse than having an inspector.

Mick was developing a good rhythmic style, and Morag was slowly gaining confidence with his lead. She managed to avoid his toes, even though it took her a while to master the reverse turn steps in the waltz.

"Don't be afraid. Rather than trying to avoid his feet when you step forwards, go between his. Like this." Annie took Mick to demonstrate and then took hold of Morag in Mick's position. "You're far less likely to get trodden on or to bump into Mick's feet if you do it like that," she reminded them. Then she put them together. "Stand a little closer and you'll find it easier." She gently moved Mick's hand onto Morag's shoulder blade.

"You're so clever, being able to dance both men's and women's steps," Morag said. "I remember now. You said that once before. Sorry."

Annie smiled. "Years of practice. And don't be sorry. It's a lot to take in all at once. It'll suddenly click, and you'll wonder how you ever got it wrong."

She was hyperaware of the gaunt figure sitting in the far corner, observing her every word, but she managed to pursue her aims for the lesson. By the end, when she glanced across the room for what seemed the zillionth time, David had vanished. She was unsure why he was there or exactly how long he had stayed. He had left as silently as he had arrived.

All the dancers agreed that the lesson had been successful, and they decided to go to the pub for a drink.

"I'm ready for a long, cool cider," Christine said.

James put his arm around her waist and said, "Me too — only make mine a long, cool lager."

Annie was gratified to see Christine smile up at her husband. Dancing was good for many things.

"Are you coming, Annie?" James called across the room.

"I'll perhaps pop in for a quick one. I'll catch you up. I need to finish packing up here, but I shan't be long. Thanks." She needed a few moments to catch her breath and calm her frayed nerves. After that, a drink would disappear down her throat in seconds, her mouth was so dry. It was wonderful that this was the first time her class had wanted to include her. It was a good sign.

Edith and Stephen were the last to leave. Annie was busy packing away her things when she overheard Edith, but she managed to continue what she was doing without turning her head. She was aware that her ears were straining.

"I've been busy. I wondered if you'd like this."

Annie gave a surreptitious glance.

Edith had produced a jar of what looked like chutney. "It's very tasty with cheese. I thought perhaps you wouldn't get much homemade food if you're on your own, now."

"That's truly kind, Edith. Not much homemade these days, you're right there."

"I like to do it, and I don't have anyone to cook for since my sister passed away. It's nothing much."

"Thank you," Stephen said. He gave Edith a peck on the cheek before putting the jar in his bag and beating a hasty retreat. "See you next week, must dash."

Edith raised her shoulders and giggled, before patting her hair. "Such a dear boy," she said to Annie. "I think he's lonely, you know. His girlfriend left him. Such a silly girl, if you ask me. She didn't know when she was well off. See you next week."

Harry appeared as Edith was closing the outside door. "All done, then?"

"Yes. Next week I'd like to start the intermediate class I spoke of. Is that going to be alright? Did David say? I know you said you'd speak to him, but I wrote him a note about it, anyway. It seemed the polite thing to do. He came in to watch this evening's lesson, but he didn't hang around and slipped away before the end. I thought he came in to say what he thought about my request."

"It's no problem at all. He told me he was happy and said it'd be on the same hourly terms."

"That's a relief. I'll contact the two couples who want to come with a reminder."

"I expect you'll have a busy weekend, then," Harry said. "What with planning new classes and…" He hesitated. "Are you going out with your new boyfriend again?"

"He's just a friend, Harry. Why do you ask?"

"Oh, well, no reason. I just want you to enjoy life and have a good time. You deserve all that. I'm happy for you."

Meeting up in the pub after the second lesson of the evening soon became a habit that Annie enjoyed. By the time she arrived, sometimes with Ted, Judy, Cameron and Gillian from the intermediate class, there was only time for one drink, but that was enough. The camaraderie of the group grew. Laughter and light-hearted banter increased. They usually commandeered the small room at the back of the rather dismal local pub. It was handy and better than travelling any distance.

Annie couldn't help but notice a deepening warmth between Christine and James. Sometimes they continued to bicker, but more often Christine gazed at her husband with adoration as he held forth on some subject or other.

"He reads a lot," Christine said once, "so he knows something about lots of things."

"A blasted know-all, you mean?" This came from Malcolm, his friend, and was taken in good part.

James threw back his head and laughed. Then he lifted his glass. "Here's to all know-alls, wherever they may be."

Mick and Morag had become an item, Annie was certain. It was heartening to see that they liked to touch each other. It might be simply her hand on his arm as she spoke, or his hand on the small of her back as their stools were pulled close together.

"I heard a joke the other day," Morag said, during a lull in the conversation.

"Go on, then," James said.

"Why do dogs... No, hang on." Morag hunched her shoulders as she thought.

Several of the group cried her name.

"Hush," Mick said. "Listen up. Give her a break."

"Why *don't* dogs make good dancers?"

Together they chorused, "I don't know. Why don't dogs..."

"Give it to us, then," James interrupted.

"Because they have two left feet. Ta-da!" Morag raised her arms and struck a pose.

There were mixed groans. Some clapped and laughed.

"Well done," Mick said and chuckled.

"You're certainly no dancing dog these days, is she Mick?" Annie said.

Mick put his arm around Morag's shoulder and kissed her cheek. "She's certainly not," he said.

Morag leaned into the embrace and smiled up at him, but a bright flush rose up her neck and suffused her cheeks.

Annie experienced a flutter inside. Those were the days. The look Morag had given Mick transported her back to the early days with Rob. The thrill of the physical closeness, the expectation and anticipation of a kiss, the wonder of being loved for who and what she was, had been so amazing. She'd thought they'd had their whole lives ahead of them and that the adventure would get better and better. Yet here she was, alone. She wondered if her Partner date, Nigel, would develop into 'the one', but she doubted it. He was too charming and full of himself. She wanted someone down to earth and caring; someone who would support her and share her interests.

Her thoughts ambled on as those around her laughed. Then she heard, "No Stephen tonight. I wonder what he gets up to." James sipped his pint.

"Out with a girl, no doubt. At his age he should be, anyway."

"I don't think he is, though. Seems a bit lonely, from what I can gather," Mick said.

Annie looked from one face to another and took it all in.

James continued, "And I think our Edith has the hots for him."

There were cries of, "Oh!" and "No way!"

"I'm telling you," James said. "You watch her next week. She giggles like a teenager and flutters her eyelashes at him."

Annie shuffled in her seat and took a cooling slurp from her glass of iced slimline tonic.

Morag, ever sensitive, glanced sideways at her and changed the subject. "We know three sequence dances now. We should have a social get-together and hire a hall one Saturday." Then she took fright when everyone looked at her and began to backtrack. "Well, just a thought."

Annie smiled at her. "I think that's a great idea. Each person could provide a small snack and you could bring your own drinks, since we don't have a licence or anything like that. What do you think?" She looked around the group.

Enthusiastic nods and agreements ensued.

"Why don't we hold it at the house? We all know the ballroom, and it's so beautiful. Surely, the owner — David, is it? — would agree?" Judy said. "Oh, but you'd have to lead it, Annie. That seems a bit of an imposition. Why don't we all pay a fiver or whatever for the hire of the room and your time?"

"I think you'd better do a proper costing and tell us how much it would be, lass," Cameron suggested.

"Okay. I'm happy to do that. I think it might be best, because there are things like caretaker time, too."

"Oh yes, I hadn't thought of all those things," Morag said. "Sorry."

"I'm sure it wouldn't come to too much, but I'll work it out and let you all know," Annie said. "I'll need to ask Harry if there are any tables anywhere. We could do with some around the edge if we're having food and drink."

"Oh dear, it's all getting complicated." Morag pushed back her hair.

"No, no, not at all. I'll get back to you. It really is a great idea."

CHAPTER 18

Annie was as excited as the students at the idea of a social dance. She could advertise it on her website, and maybe some new people would be interested. Perhaps she could even inform the sequence dance group who met in the city. If she was charging a small admission fee, it would be another income source.

While she drove to the house the next morning, Annie was in a state of nervous anticipation, hoping that Harry and David would be at home and that David would accept her suggestion.

She thought about Stephen. It would be great if she could get another partner for him, especially if others were noticing Edith's crush. The problem then would be Edith. Annie didn't want to lose her. She was probably lonely too, since her sister had died, and she clearly enjoyed the dancing classes. This was getting complicated. Was it really her place to become involved in the private lives of her students? Probably not, as she had her own life to sort out.

This thing with Nigel wasn't going anywhere. He was pleasant enough but, to be honest, he wasn't her type. He was too smooth, too aware of his own image — not in an under-confident way like Harry, but in a presumptuous, brash manner. In fact, the more she considered him, the less she wanted to meet him again. Would she email, phone or what? It was a bit cowardly to text. Perhaps she would call.

Her thoughts turned to Partner.com. Should she try again? She might yet meet Mr Right — someone kind, who would consider her as Rob had done. Only now she needed a man who didn't mind her showing a flash of independence with her new business. Yes, Partner.com might be the way forward. She'd tried it once, and it wasn't as scary as she'd imagined.

Annie arrived at Moondreams House when the worst of the black clouds had moved across the sky to deposit their load on some other poor souls. She parked her car and skittered across the gritty surface of the courtyard, jumping a couple of puddles before arriving at the door she had used previously with Harry. Sure she could hear movement inside, she knocked on the frosted glass pane.

"Comin'." A voice came from within, and Mrs M eventually pulled back the bolt and opened the door. "Oh, 'ello. It's you. Come in, me duck," she said. "Wanna cuppa tea? I was makin' one."

"Thank you. That'd be lovely." Annie knew it was important to get this lady onside. She probably had David's ear almost as much as Harry did.

"Sit yerself down, then."

Annie hung her jacket over the back of the chair and did as she was bid. "I was hoping I might have a quick word with Mr Troughton."

"Oh." Mrs M paused while she made the tea, and Annie became nervous again with the silence. "Right. I thought you must have come to see 'Arry. David, is it? Oh."

Annie was very tempted to say what she wanted to see David about but resisted, since she didn't know what his reaction would be.

"What's it about, then?" Mrs M asked.

"I need to ask him about an idea."

Mrs M's shoulders twitched. She was clearly miffed that Annie wasn't more forthcoming.

"You do a grand job, looking after Mr Troughton," Annie said, trying to change the subject.

"I do me best. It's not easy, I can tell you."

"I'm sure," Annie said. "He'll be a little set in his ways, I expect. I'm sure he's pleased to have you here, though."

She seemed mollified. "Right, miss. Shall I tell 'im you're 'ere?"

"Thank you.." She took another slurp from her mug of tea.

Mrs M disappeared and Annie looked around the kitchen. It was old-fashioned but clean enough. Mrs M seemed more conscientious in this area. Minutes later, Annie heard footsteps. She stood in preparation and tried to organise her thoughts. She was still on edge about meeting David, especially since he had watched part of her lesson, when she was certain he must have been judging her competence. However, it wasn't David but Harry who came into the kitchen.

A beaming smile lit up his face. "Hello. I didn't realise you were here."

"I came to ask David something. The classes wondered if we could have a social dance either one Saturday evening or on a Sunday afternoon. What do you think?" Annie whispered the last bit as she leaned towards Harry. Then she straightened with a jerk. "Have you lost weight?" She suddenly realised he looked so much more trim, despite his baggy, scruffy work clothes.

Harry flattened his hands across his stomach in a self-conscious gesture. "Er, well. Yes. Quite a bit. I've been meaning to," he added hastily. "I'm not ill or anything." He chuckled, shrugged his shoulders, and turned away towards the kettle. "Do you want one?" He indicated the teapot.

Was he avoiding her gaze? "Mrs M made me one. She's gone to find David for me."

"How are things? I haven't seen you for a bit. I've been busy, and so have you, I imagine, what with the dance classes and Nigel. Is that his name?"

"Yes, but I don't…"

"Good morning, Mrs Ellis." David stalked into the room with Mrs M behind him. "You wanted to see me, I understand. Shall we go through to my study, if it's business we are discussing?" Then he turned to Harry. "Did you manage to finish that job? Perhaps you would look at my bathroom tap. It's developed quite a drip. After your break, of course. Thank you, Mrs M. Don't let me keep you. I'm sure you are busy."

With that, David indicated that Annie should precede him from the room and head towards the large open hall. With a last glance over her shoulder at Harry, who was watching her, she left the kitchen. In the hall, David opened a door that led to a dark, wood-panelled room. Bookshelves lined one wall and a large, heavy-looking oak desk sat against another, with a high-backed brown leather chair before it. There was a small cast-iron fireplace with a black marble hearth and a brass fender, and a pair of small tapestry chairs stood on either side. David indicated that they should sit on these. Annie perched on the edge of hers while David sat back and crossed his long legs. Resting his elbows on the fine polished arms, he laced his long fingers together in front of him. With his chin on his chest, he regarded her from under his brows.

Annie forced herself to sit back. It felt like an interview for an important job, but she would not be intimidated by this man. She took a deep breath. "Were you interested in my dance class? I saw you came to watch a couple of weeks ago." She scrutinised his face for a reaction, forgetting her apprehensiveness.

David uncrossed his legs and shifted his position. "I was interested to see how it was going," he responded.

"Do you dance?" Most men of his age seemed to have learned in their youth, Annie thought.

"Yes. My … er … wife, my late wife and I used to dance quite frequently. We went several times to Just Dance — to social dances, not lessons."

"I didn't realise," Annie said. "Actually, it's that kind of thing I've come to speak to you about." She took another deep breath and plunged on. "Several of my students are more experienced dancers, and the beginners have learned several little routines now as well as a few sequence dances." She paused. "They were asking if we might have a social dance." She told him of her initial ideas.

David folded his arms. "A Sunday afternoon would suit, to begin with. How many do you anticipate coming? Are you opening it up to others?"

"The students I have would only add up to less than twenty people. I wondered about inviting the people in the sequence dance club in the city."

David stuck his bottom lip out in contemplation, rested his elbows on the armrests and steepled his fingers against his chin. "I see."

"I don't have a firm date yet, but it will be within the next couple of months. I'd want to co-ordinate with the sequence dance club. I wouldn't want to choose a date they already have booked. I can look on their website for that. Of course, I'd pay you to use the room, and Harry to clean, especially since I'd be charging a nominal amount for tickets the first time."

"The first time! Is this to be a regular thing, then?"

"Well…" Annie lost her courage. "We'd have to see, I suppose."

"The ones we used to go to on a Sunday afternoon were tea dances, with a hot drink and a cake halfway through. You'd be expected to provide that."

"Yes." Annie thought on her feet. "I could get a water urn and set all that up on a table at the end of the ballroom. I'd have to hire cups, saucers and plates."

"Oh, we've got all that. From years ago." David waved his hand dismissively. "It'll all need a jolly good clean, I imagine."

Annie could not believe it. He had mentioned the tableware so casually. He almost sounded like he was becoming enthused about the idea.

"We better discuss a hire charge," he said.

After her meeting with David, Annie crossed the cavernous entrance hall in a euphoric state. Sun streamed through the huge windows, striping the worn rug and emphasising the rich colours that were left. It could not have gone better. Already her mind was buzzing with plans. She wanted to rush home and start to sort out the finer details.

When she got back to the kitchen, Harry was nowhere to be seen. He'd presumably gone to sort out the dripping tap. Mrs M was stirring something in the large pan she had placed earlier. Annie hoped it tasted better than it smelled.

"Hi," Annie said as she retrieved her jacket from the back of the chair.

"Hello, duck, everything alright? Did you manage to discuss whatever it was?"

"Yes, thank you. David has agreed that I can run a tea dance in the ballroom, one Sunday afternoon soon."

It wouldn't hurt for Mrs M to spread the word now, as she was bound to do. It would be useful, in fact.

"Say cheerio to Harry for me, would you? I'll give him a call soon. I shall need to make sure he can be around on the afternoon I decide, so I'll have to consult with him for a suitable date."

"Righty-o, me duck. Safe journey."

Annie guessed that she was making an ally there.

On the way home, she decided to make a short detour and called into the teashop. Making enough cakes would be way beyond her capabilities, and anyway, they would need to conform with all the food hygiene regulations. It would be good business for Sarah at the Little Teapot Café.

When Annie proposed the idea, the woman's enthusiasm bubbled over.

"Wow! Fantastic. Can I advertise that I've made the cakes?" Sarah asked. "It would do my business no end of good." Her broad face wore a grin that was infectious, and Annie smiled back, readily agreeing to set up an A-frame blackboard at the side of the serving table.

"This is my assistant, Natalie," Sarah said as a young lady came from the kitchen. "She could help," Sarah said.

Annie arrived home full of anticipation and nerves as a new thought struck her. She would need servers to help with teas. She couldn't possibly do all that and lead the dancing. What about Ginny? She smiled to herself. She loved Ginny, but she was a little clumsy. Oh Lord, who could she ask? Would Si do it? She had so few friends now, and all those refusals of invitations were coming back to bite her. Ellie. Ellie might do it. She was of an age to welcome the money, and it wouldn't interfere with her social life or her studies on a Sunday afternoon. Feeling better, Annie turned her thoughts to Nigel and whether she should try Partner.com again.

"What do you think, Raffa?" She reached down to the side of her chair and stroked her dog's ear, then picked up her phone. Should she text or call Nigel? It was cowardly to write a rejection, but she hadn't had to handle this sort of thing for many years. In the end, she dialled Nigel's number.

Once the greetings were out of the way, she launched straight in. "Nigel, about going out on Friday." She took a deep breath and squeezed her eyes shut. "I'm ringing to call it off."

"Oh dear. Okay, well, we can rearrange. What about Saturday? That might be better for me anyway."

Annie raised her eyes and cursed herself. She hadn't been clear enough. "No, I mean … well, I mean call it off, the whole thing." Annie gritted her teeth and winced.

"Are we done, then?" There was a pause.

"Er. Yes, I guess we are. Thank you for the times we went out, but I don't think it's going to work for me."

"Your loss, lady. Or perhaps I should just say, your loss." The line went dead.

Annie tossed her phone down on her lap. The implication of his final words had left her shaking. Perhaps she should have texted. She had phoned because she considered herself well-mannered and polite, but he'd implied she was no lady. Well then, better out of it, for sure.

She retrieved her phone and called Ginny.

"His loss, more like," her friend said when Annie described the previous call. "He's probably not used to rejection. Arrogant sod, is all. You're better off without."

"I suppose I hurt his feelings," Annie said.

"Don't be put off. Mr Impeccable is out there. Get back on the horse, as they say."

"Thanks, Ginny. Sleep well."

"See you soon, girl."

That seems like good advice, Annie thought, and she loaded the Partner website on her laptop. *No time like the present.* Her trembling continued as she looked at who was there. It still seemed an unromantic way to go about dating, but every date would be a learning experience. At best she might meet someone special and at worst she would discover new things, perhaps gaining a little confidence again on the way.

As she scrolled she came across a firefighter who thought he had a great physique and an ex-naval lieutenant who wanted to be a patisserie chef. That could be useful. However, when Annie read what he wrote about a cherry, dry nuts, and ganache-ing buns, she moved on with haste. Next came a guy who asked about favourite books and said his was the *Kama Sutra*. No way. She also avoided those who were 'just passing through' the city. She had no interest in a one night stand. Eventually she came across someone who sounded more promising, although he said that he was probably boring. Straight away, her interest was piqued. She wasn't looking for a go-getter, a jetsetter. Homely, kind, and supportive was more her type.

Annie read on. William's interests were walking and birdwatching. He could be dull, but she wasn't going to judge yet. He had a daughter in her early twenties. Alright. She could probably cope with an adult. It wasn't like trying to get little ones onside. He said he was lacking in self-esteem but was getting used to exploring new activities, and he had tried archery, sequence dancing with his daughter and golf. Sequence dancing. Well, well.

Annie swiped right.

"Now we wait and see," she said to Raffa.

CHAPTER 19

Harry was in turmoil. Annie had noticed his new svelte self, but David had entered the room before he'd had a chance to find out how her relationship with 'the charmer' was going. He swerved from feeling confident about forming a connection with Annie to being dashed down and fearful again. He could handle new love, probably, even though he'd been rubbish in the past. What if she wanted children? That was the real issue. Could he risk it? No. Not a second time. Life was so complicated.

"Did Annie say why she came?" Harry asked Mrs M over a bowl of savoury mince and mashed potatoes. He forked his spuds a little more to get rid of the residual lumps, and so was able to avoid her eyes. David had a tray in his rooms, so they were free to talk.

"Ooh, yes. Well, no, but she told me after she'd spoken with 'im." She tossed her head in the direction of David's rooms upstairs. "She wants to run a dance thing. Some social, one Sunday afternoon. I was amazed — apparently 'e said yes to the idea."

"That's good. Maybe it could be the making of him, and the house, to get some life back into things."

"I know. 'E was talking of finding a buyer again, only the other day. Don't know who'd want this old pile, mind."

"I suppose someone could turn it into a hotel or something."

"Oh Gawd, I never thought o' that. Blimey, it's not much of a job here, but it suits me, and you'd be out of an 'ome. Out on the streets."

Harry's stomach swooped at the reminder of his perilous position. "Perhaps we need to start a covert offensive and subtly persuade him to get involved in this dancing thing. He used to dance regularly when Jane was alive."

Later that day, Harry stopped his sweeping and stood staring up at the ceiling in the ballroom. He was sure that spider of brown was creeping further across. There were no drips on the floor, but the rain earlier had been heavy. It must have been raining for most of the night, judging by the puddles in the courtyard. He hoped there weren't any puddles lying among the slats above the plaster. It must dry out between rainstorms, but damage would be occurring.

The door opened behind him and David entered the room.

"Look at this." Harry raised his eyes to the stain. "I'm sure it's got worse."

"You contacted people for quotes for the main roof, did you?"

"Yes. A couple of companies have been. One of them seemed a right cowboy outfit, but Heritage Roofing are coming tomorrow. They're specialists in lead work as well as our type of stone slates."

"Better get them to look at this roof too."

Harry raised his eyebrows, surprised that David seemed willing to spend money.

"I know what I said. It'll need someone who knows what they're doing, though."

"While you're here, David, would you show me a dance step I'm struggling with?" Harry asked.

"Why didn't you ask Mrs Ellis, Annie, earlier? She would have shown you."

"I was busy, so I didn't see her getting ready to leave, and then it was too late."

David sighed. "What is it?"

"I've been trying to teach myself a thing called a hesitation, whisk and chassé in the waltz. I've been learning from a DVD I bought, but this bit is hard to follow."

"Really? That's a fairly basic step. Come on, then." David grimaced.

He performed the steps and Harry copied him.

"Let me watch you," David said.

After a couple of goes, David sighed again. "You need to relax your knees as you step forward and lead with your heel. Then rise on your toes. The rise and fall will give you better flow. You'll feel the music and that'll help. Then up on toes for the chassé. After that, you'll step outside your partner."

"Ah, that's where I'm going wrong, I expect. You couldn't do the woman's part, could you?"

"Oh, Harry, really?"

"Go on. There's no one to see."

"Come here, then." David held his arms out and Harry stepped in, feeling embarrassed and foolish but determined to get the steps correct and to involve David. It was a two-pronged attack.

They did a couple of routines around the ballroom. David reminded Harry of the rise and fall motion before breaking away. "There. That's more than enough tomfoolery for one day."

"Thank you. That was great and really helpful. Truly."

"You need to get yourself some proper lessons, Harry."

"Yes, I will. Soon. Maybe." That would have been easier if his timing in asking Annie out properly had not been slapped down by Nigel showing up. Now, although Harry was continuing with his grand plan, he was full of anxious low self-esteem again.

CHAPTER 20

"A dance, whoop! That's excellent news," the older students chorused at the next lesson.

"Good show," Edith said to Annie. "Well done you, for getting it off the ground so promptly."

"I still need to verify a date," said Annie. "I'm waiting for the teacher of the sequence dance group in town to get back to me. I don't want to clash with her. Some of her students may want to come. Would that be a problem? It might make for a better atmosphere to have a few more people."

"They'll know a lot more than us. They might swamp us," Morag said and looked worried.

"It might all be a bit easy for them. They might be bored," Christine said.

"I can do a programme that will suit everyone, I'm sure." Annie tried to sound confident. It was certainly not beyond her capabilities. However, it was a long time since she'd been involved in organising anything like this. "I'll make sure there are plenty of items and variety for all of you," she said, trying to reassure herself as much as them.

"Have you heard from Stephen?" Edith was looking around.

"I haven't, no," Annie said.

"I do hope he's alright." Edith looked worried now. "I haven't anyone to dance with."

"I'll partner you," Annie assured her. "We'll manage. I'm sure he'll arrive soon. Right, let's pick up where we left off last time. I'll put some music on and then we'll have a quick reminder of the hesitation, whisk and chassé in the waltz."

As they danced around the room with their reverse and natural turns, one or two couples had a go at the new steps. Annie was leading Edith while keeping half an eye on them all and shouting out encouragement and reminders about heel leads and using toes for a rise and fall. She was so engrossed that she didn't notice the internal door open and quietly close again. When the music stopped and her students turned to her for instruction, Annie was surprised to see that David had come in and was already seated in his previous position against the far wall.

Immediately, her heart gave its customary lurch.

She began to remind the class of their steps for the new sequence and was about to take Edith for the practice when she had an idea.

If she could encourage David to become the smallest bit involved, it could have major benefits for him and this house. She decided to go across to him and have a quiet word. Again, he waved her away as he had done previously, but this time she took a deep breath and ploughed on.

"Have a little try on your own. I'll only be a minute," she called over her shoulder to the class.

With each step towards David, Annie's heart thumped harder. She cleared her throat, hoping it would stop her mouth feeling so dry. As she approached, David unfolded his long body and limbs and stood, towering over her.

Annie gulped. "Mr Troughton. David." She stuck out her hand and because he couldn't do anything else, he shook it politely.

"Mrs Ellis. Annie."

Annie gave herself a mental shake. David must have enjoyed dancing at one time, when he'd gone with his wife to social dances. He might even do something about the awful state of the ceiling in this magnificent room.

"I'm one down tonight." She nodded back at her students. "I wondered if I might prevail upon you to dance for a few moments with Edith. We're learning a new step, you see, and I understand you used to dance a lot."

"Well, I…"

"Only for this part of my lesson. I wouldn't ask if it was something insignificant. I really would be incredibly grateful. It's a new step, you see." Annie managed to stop talking before she repeated herself anymore. She stood her ground and maintained eye contact.

David compressed his lips and breathed out a gust of air. "Very well," he said after a moment.

Edith stood to one side and was gallantly trying the steps on her own.

"Madam," David said. "May I? It seems I might be of help." He looked across at Annie with a piercing and unsmiling gaze.

She had a moment of terror. Had she made the most gigantic error?

David did not stay beyond that part of the lesson. He approached Annie as they finished their waltz.

"I hope that sufficed," he said to her before he left.

"Thank you so much. Yes."

"The lady dances well. What was her name?"

"She's Edith Hill." Then Annie added quietly, "Her sister passed away. They lived together, so she's enjoying these classes now she's on her own."

"Lovely lady." With that he inclined his head to Edith, nodded at Annie and was gone, leaving Annie totally unsure whether she had overplayed her hand or not. She must ask

Harry later, if she saw him at all. He seemed elusive these days. She was unsure why. She hoped they were still friends.

Both classes were finished, and the second group were preparing to leave for the pub. Annie told them she was going straight home this time. She would check her text messages in a minute and see if there was anything from Stephen. She hoped he was alright.

She also needed to check her emails to see if the sequence dance leader had responded. She wanted to look at her Partner.com account, too, although she wasn't holding out much hope for that. Perhaps she should try and get a few different dates and enjoy the experience of going out. It shouldn't be too serious.

When her phone pinged, Annie was relieved. It was a text from Stephen. He apologised for the late notice, but he'd had car trouble and he promised he'd be there the following week by any means necessary. As Annie packed away her things, her eyes kept straying to the internal door. She hoped David wouldn't return right now, but she did hope to see Harry. She would ask him if he had seen David and whether he'd said anything about her, following her virtually browbeating him into helping Edith.

She was distracted by her phone pinging again in her pocket. It was a message from William: *Pleased to have received your details. Shall we meet?*

"Oh, my goodness," Annie said aloud, distracted from all else by the message.

"Good news, I hope," said Harry behind her, throwing her into confusion.

"I have another date," she said, holding up her phone.

Harry looked surprised. "Oh? What about that guy Nigel?"

"I knocked him back. He wasn't my type. Too much of a charmer. Arrogant and showy. I need someone more…" She thought for a moment. "More homely. He thought more of himself and the impression he was creating than of me or anything else."

"I didn't take to him," Harry said. "If he was like that at the beginning … well." He shrugged. "Who's this other guy?"

"He sounds much nicer." Annie told him what little she knew.

"And will you meet him?"

Harry sounded a bit grumpy, Annie thought. "I guess so. Not much point plucking up the courage to join a dating site and then not following through, I suppose."

"Possibly. I can't see why you are doing it at all, Annie."

"I need to get out again. Ginny said…"

"Oh! Ginny said … well!"

Annie was taken aback so decided to change the subject. "David came in tonight and danced with one of my students. Has he mentioned it?"

"How on earth did you manage that?"

Annie explained the gist of what had happened.

"It could be the saving of David and the house. I mean, look at it." Harry gestured towards the ceiling. "I'm sure it's getting worse. I've organised some quotes for the work. Need to persuade the master to put his hand in his pocket for it. If he would take an interest in the dancing, Mrs M and I were saying earlier, it might help."

"Your position would be safer too."

"Yes, exactly. We would all benefit."

"I was worried I'd upset him," Annie said.

"He seemed upbeat about it. I passed him in the hall as he was coming away from here. It was only a brief conversation. He said Edith was a lovely lady, but that's all."

"That sounds okay, doesn't it?" Annie needed the reassurance.

"Yes, perhaps we could, between us, arrange for something similar again. It would be a conspiracy." Harry grinned, at ease again, it seemed.

Annie didn't want to lose this friendship. These days, he looked so much more together and on top of things. They always chatted easily, and Harry had been so helpful and considerate.

CHAPTER 21

Ginny gasped in air and blew it out like a habitual smoker. Her forehead was shiny, and her neck and shoulders were pink. Annie and she were powerwalking around the park.

"I think we'd better take a break," Annie said. "Let's get to the bench by the lake, and that'll be enough for today."

"Right. Good idea. We could … go into the watersports … centre and get a nice … long latte."

"No point walking and then putting all the calories back in." Annie laughed. "Drink your water," she added, which earned her a dour look.

"Yes, you're right. A spoilsport … but right."

As Ginny collapsed onto the bench, she pulled at her bright pink Lycra top and said, "Look at this. It's so tight these days. I'm sure it used to fit better when I bought it." She paused. "So what's with this William guy?"

"He seemed really nice. A bit shy and uncertain. Very attentive, but not in a self-aware way. I mean, he's not trying to show off. Certainly not another Nigel the Cocky."

Ginny took a swig from her water bottle. "Well? Tell me more."

"He's lovely. Particularly good-looking, as it happens, but totally unaware of it. He's been married, too. Got a daughter who's twenty-one."

"How old is he, then?"

"He put forty-one on his profile. That must be about right. Right age for me, too. He said he was married quite young, but only for a couple of years."

"If he's got a daughter who's twenty-one, he must have been very young when he got married. Perhaps his father-in-law had the shotgun polished and ready."

"It didn't sound like it. I gathered he was more than ready to leave home and set up on his own. Sounded like his own dad was really strict."

"So, what happened to the wife? She's not under the patio, I take it?"

Annie grinned. "No, his wife left and remarried, but they still seem to be friends and he sees her and Natalie, his daughter, quite often. He tried sequence dancing with his daughter. Can you believe it? How amazing is that? They must get on quite well."

"He didn't keep going to lessons?"

"I suppose not. Still…"

"So, who has he been with since his marriage broke up?"

"That's the odd part. No one."

"No one? Not at all?"

"He says not."

"Blimey! What's he after with you, then?"

"Hot sex and a model-shaped girlfriend who's an ace in the kitchen, obviously." Annie laughed.

"I'm serious. Why now after all this time of, presumably, celibacy?"

"I did ask him the same, actually. He says he's frightened of being lonely in old age. It was rather sad. He's got a reasonable job in insurance, he's got a small house with a garden, he runs a modest car, but he says he has no one with whom to watch and talk about TV programmes, nobody to go to the cinema with, or to take out for dinner. He said he can't keep asking his daughter. It's not natural for her to be hanging out with her dad."

"Didn't he mention the 's' word, then?"

"Sex? No, not at all."

"Very strange."

"We'll see. It was refreshing and wonderfully comfortable and nice. Come on, then." Annie bounced up. "Enough of this talk."

"Hold on. Not so fast. Are you seeing him again?"

"Yes. We're going to the cinema on Friday evening and then for a curry."

"There won't be much snogging in the back row, by the sound of it."

"We'll see," Annie said again. "He did hold my hand last time, and his was warm and comforting. That was when he saw me back to my car. Then it was a chaste kiss on the cheek."

"It all sounds a little brotherly."

"There was a frisson of … something. On my part. I don't know about him, of course. I felt safe."

"Ooh, well, that's promising, I suppose."

The following Tuesday, Harry stood at the door of the ballroom as Annie put the last of her things into her bag.

"Was it a good session?" He picked up her other bag to carry it to the car for her.

"It was. Any move on the David front?" Annie followed him to the door.

"He was asking about the social dance. How're the preparations coming along?"

"I've got cakes organised. Sarah at the Little Teapot Café is doing them. Ginny's daughter, Ellie, and her friend are going to come and plate them up and serve the teas and coffees. I've heard back from the leader of the sequence dance group. She was happy that I'd contacted her, and she'll pass on the date to her group. They'll contact me directly if they want tickets. I can do all that from home. I've sorted the date, and David said it's okay. I gather he mentioned something to you."

"Yes, the date's fine for me too. I'm happy to be around to make sure there's no trouble."

"So, I've got four weeks to advertise it and get everything ready. Ooh, yes, I nearly forgot, David said there was a cupboard with cups and saucers. I need to ask you if I can see those. I bet they need washing before the day."

"I'll show you now, if you like. Let's put this in your car and we'll go back." As they walked across the courtyard towards the kitchen, Harry asked, "How's the dating thing going?" He was pleased with himself for sounding affable. Last time he was edgy, and he sensed Annie had picked up on it because she'd changed the subject too quickly.

Now he had to endure her telling him how nice this William guy was. Why had he even asked? Talk about salt in wounds.

Harry didn't know what he wanted. Well, he did. He wanted Annie, but he still couldn't risk it. He couldn't allow himself to.

"You're looking very trim these days, Harry."

He missed what she'd said. "Sorry?"

"I said you're looking very fit. Slim," Annie added with haste. "Have you lost weight? And you've got new clothes, haven't you?"

Fit! Did she say fit? "Er … yes. I've lost a couple of stones. I had to buy several new things. Everything I had was hanging off, even with a belt for my trousers. They were all baggy at the back. I'm assured that wearing trousers with a drooping crotch is not a good look."

Annie wondered who had told him that. "I'm pleased for you. I'm really glad you're getting back on track. Is there someone special in your life these days? That's often why people get smartened up."

"There is a lady I like. I like her a lot."

"Oh, Harry. That's marvellous. Tell me more."

"No." He laughed, suddenly self-conscious. No way would he confess how much he loved *her*. Especially not when she had been raving about this William. "Er … it's … um… It's early days," he prevaricated.

"Okay. I do wish you well, though."

Saved by the cups and saucers, Harry thought as they arrived in the kitchen and he strode across to one of the large cupboards beside the Aga. He opened the door with an exaggerated flourish. "Ta-da," he sang, trying to cover his confusion.

Fortunately, Annie was distracted. "Wow! Why are there so many?"

"We used to have great gatherings in the ballroom when Jane was alive. There's an urn for hot water too, and cutlery in that box."

"When David said I could use them, I had no idea there would be so much. It's perfect." On impulse Annie stood on tiptoe, stretched up and kissed Harry's cheek. Then she stepped back. "Sorry. Didn't mean to embarrass you. It's so exciting, and you've been such a good friend. Thank you, Harry."

Friend! That's still how she sees me, he thought. *My own fault, I suppose, for hanging back when I might have had the chance.*

CHAPTER 22

The scene was set. Tables at one end of the ballroom were covered with powder-blue cloths to match the ceiling. Annie had spent some of the morning helping Harry put out chairs from the storeroom, so that people could sit and watch others when they weren't dancing.

Ellie and her friend, Liv, had got into the spirit of the occasion and wore smart black trousers and white shirts. Annie hadn't asked them to dress as such, but she was happy. "You look great, girls," she said. "Thank you so much."

Despite being nonchalant teenagers, both girls grinned and looked suitably pleased with themselves.

"I don't think you'll need to start cutting and plating the cakes until about two forty-five. We don't want them to dry out. I'm planning to serve tea and cake at three-thirty, and if we switch the urn on when people start to arrive that'll allow plenty of time for it to heat up."

"They're all coming at two, is that right?" Liv asked.

"Yes. I sold thirty-six tickets in the end, which was more than I was expecting for the first time. All those people coming from the sequence dance club is amazing. Their leader was ever so helpful, and she told me some of the new dances they've learned. Then there'll be all the old favourites, plus the few I've taught my lot."

"It sounds quite exciting, doesn't it, Liv?" Ellie nudged her friend.

"Yeah! Will they wear all those big floaty dresses?"

"No." Annie laughed. "Probably just smart afternoon stuff. Maybe if we had an evening dance, the ladies would be more dressed up. We'll see how this goes first. Eventually I thought we could have a dressy do where the men wear their suits, and the women will have a chance to wear their finery."

"Ooh, yeah! Maybe for a celebration like Halloween. It could be an orange and black theme, or perhaps you could hold it when Christmas comes. I'd be up for helping at that. Wouldn't you, Ellie?"

"Let's not get carried away," Annie said. "As I say, we'll see how this one goes first. I think I heard a car."

The outside door opened, and two couples came in. Annie didn't know them, so she assumed they were from the club in town. The two men showed their tickets and Annie tore them while wearing her best smile and welcoming them.

"Where shall we hang our coats?"

Annie took a breath. She hadn't thought of that. "I hope they'll be alright on the backs of your chairs, or you could lay them over there," she said, pointing to the old benches along the wall.

"Oh, that's fine," the other lady said. Before they went to sit down and change into their dance shoes, another lot arrived.

Annie was so busy taking tickets that she didn't see William behind them with a young woman. "I hope this is alright," he said as his turn to enter came.

"Hello." Annie's surprise must have shown in her voice.

"Can we pay on the door? If it's a problem, not to worry. We can go. This is Natalie, my daughter."

"Oh! Hello. We met at Sarah's café. Those are your cakes." Annie laughed. She did a quick mental calculation. There would be enough cake and there were a few cups left in the box under the table. "Of course. How wonderful to see you again, Natalie."

"We're very rusty, of course," Natalie said, "but, let's go and give it a try…"

Oh my gosh, Annie thought. *No pressure here, then, meeting the new boyfriend's daughter when I'm hosting an event.* "Great to have you both here," she managed.

They moved on into the room to make way for others.

Some of Annie's students arrived within the next few minutes.

"This looks marvellous," Christine said.

"Aye, you've done a first-rate job here, lass," Cameron McKay added as he and Gillian followed Christine and James into the hall. Annie immediately felt more relaxed.

Edith arrived next. "Is Stephen here?"

"Not yet, but I do know he's coming," Annie said.

"Jolly good. I'll go and bag us a couple of chairs."

Annie winced internally.

Stephen arrived after some more people that Annie didn't know. "I'm a bit nervous about this," he confessed.

"You're not the only one," Annie said. "I've been pacing half the night, and when I wasn't busy this morning I could think of little else. I so want it to be a success."

"It will be. Look at all these people."

"They all seem very easy-going," Annie said. "Our group is over there." She pointed to the tables where all her students were changing shoes or getting water bottles out.

"Right-o." Stephen left her to head across to the others.

Annie glanced at her watch. There were still a few people to arrive, she surmised from the number of tickets she'd sold. Five minutes to go.

Another couple arrived.

Three minutes to go.

Ted and Judy Brown opened the door, followed by Mick and Morag, who looked lovely in a full-skirted green dress. It set off her slim figure and auburn curls perfectly.

"You look lovely," Annie said.

Morag touched her hair with a self-conscious, nervous expression.

"Come on, you'll be fine," Mick said, clearly picking up on her apprehension. He put his arm around her waist and guided her across the room.

One minute.

Annie picked up the microphone. She managed to take a deep breath and steady her voice. "Hello everyone. Thank you for coming, and thank you to David Troughton, who owns the house, for allowing us to be here. We have a mixed selection today, because of our varying levels of experience. Some of you have been learning sequence dances for a long time, and others have only been coming to lessons for a matter of weeks. There are some who are learning straight ballroom and Latin, too, as well as beginning some sequences, so it'll be a variety this afternoon. We'll start off, of course, with a quickstep."

There was a general scraping of chairs and some conversation as people organised themselves. Annie put on the music.

Not everyone got up. Some of the visitors from town remained seated, as did Mick and Morag, even though Annie had taught them the basic steps. She was pleased to see all her other students having a go. Trying not to watch William all the time, Annie was impressed to note that he and Natalie were doing basic steps around the room with exceptionally good rhythm and footwork. As they passed her, William gave a beaming smile and promptly went wrong, but he managed to laugh it off and took up the steps again.

He's such a nice man, Annie thought.

As the dance finished, one or two better dancers were puffing, having cantered around the room at a great pace, avoiding those who were less experienced. Everyone seemed to be smiling or greeting each other.

The afternoon continued with a mix of straight dancing and sequences. After three or four, William approached Annie and asked if she would dance the Rumba sequence with him.

"Thank you," she said. When she'd put the music on, he took her right hand and led her very nicely into the first basic step and turn under his arm. "You dance better than you led me to believe. How long were you learning for?"

"It was about a year. We gave up because Natalie's hours changed and they clashed.."

Annie looked across to where they'd been seated, but Natalie wasn't there. Casually glancing around the room, she spotted William's daughter dancing with Stephen. Her eyes darted to the table where Edith sat with Cameron and Gillian for company, but the older woman's eyes followed Stephen as he danced. She appeared to be hardly listening to whatever Gillian was saying.

I must keep an eye on this, Annie thought. However, at teatime, Stephen escorted Edith to the table. While she chose two plates of cakes, he got the teas for them both.

Annie worked the tables, chatting to those she didn't know, asking a question here, complimenting there, gleaning information, and starting to get a feel for the people who had come. Overall, everyone seemed happy with the programme she had put together. One or two made requests for dances and she made a note to include those before the afternoon finished.

After tea, there was a mix of more advanced sequence dances as well as the easier ones Annie had taught her classes, and these were interspersed with straight ballroom and Latin numbers to which all could dance at whatever level they had achieved. Annie continued to mingle with all the visitors and students alike. She avoided dancing with William. This was a work engagement for her, and although she was enjoying the afternoon, she didn't want to be too distracted.

However, during the last half hour, Annie shared a Sweetheart Waltz sequence with William. Step point, step point and a clockwise box. His right arm was warm around her back and his hand on her shoulder blade was comforting as they repeated the initial sequence. Four quarter turns. "One, two, three; one, two, three," she heard him mumbling in her ear.

At that moment, the internal door opened and David and Harry entered the ballroom.

Annie's heart thumped as she watched over William's shoulder. Harry looked so different. His hair had been trimmed into a modern style, his figure was tall and lean and he was dressed in clothes that suited him, emphasising his broad shoulders and slim hips. How had she not noticed all this sooner? His blue eyes locked on hers and her smile faded. She became awkward and hot in William's arms, and she was puzzled about why she wished for the dance to be over.

She broke away just before the end with the excuse that she needed to be prepared to announce the next dance and change the music.

David approached one or two people and smiled and nodded. He was as gaunt as ever, but when he smiled his face showed animation and the light he exuded was given back many times over. It was a pleasure for Annie to witness.

Presumably, some of these people were from his past dancing days.

Harry stood inside the door and didn't move. Annie gave him a small, self-conscious wave, which he returned by lifting a stiff hand in front of his chest. Every so often she glanced his way, hyperaware of his presence.

Glancing at her watch, Annie picked up the microphone and said, "Well, everyone, thank you for coming. Again, thank you to David Troughton for allowing us to use this beautiful ballroom." She indicated David and, spontaneously, everyone clapped. He inclined his head graciously and smiled. It lit up his face, and Annie glowed with satisfaction. "And now, it's time for the last waltz, so please take your partners."

Annie had trouble preventing her lower jaw from dropping as she saw David approach Edith. The older lady nodded and touched her hair, which caused Annie to forget her own moment of bashful confusion. Out of the corner of her eye she saw Stephen, thus released, make a beeline for Natalie. This was all working out unexpectedly well.

She was disappointed to see William heading in the direction of the toilets. *No last dance for me*, she thought. *Oh well...*

Just then, she was startled by a voice over her shoulder. Harry stood before her as she turned from putting on the music. "Shall we?" His hand was outstretched, and he looked sheepish.

"Sorry?" Annie looked up at him blankly.

"Shall we dance? It'll be basic." He grinned and the dimple appeared.

Johnny Mathis and Henry Mancini sang and played the old-fashioned love song, 'The Sweetheart Tree' as Annie stepped into Harry's arms for the second time in her life. The music drifted around her head and through every part of her.

Then her mind was buzzing again. What was going on here? Harry was a friend, a helper, a confidant, yet she was aware of a zinging in each nerve as they glided around. Then rationale took over. He was dancing and doing it well. There was a flow to his rhythm and after the first few steps he danced with confidence, leading her own movements. Annie tipped her head back and looked up, but Harry avoided her gaze.

"Harry…"

The music was coming to an end. Harry bent his head and kissed her lips lightly. It wasn't the fumbling kiss of all those years ago, but light and assured. Annie looked up into his blue eyes. He smiled gently down at her but said nothing as he turned and strode back across the hall, leaving her with a thumping heart and a spark of something strange throughout her body.

CHAPTER 23

At the end of the event, Ellie and Liv took the boxes full of used cups and saucers to the kitchen to wash them. Harry had helped to carry them away. He hadn't approached Annie since the last dance, and she was busy anyway, saying thank you, receiving praise and sending dancers on their way. David had disappeared as silently as he had come, and all but one or two couples had left. William was standing next to Annie as she put the last of her things into her bag.

"Where's Natalie? Is she waiting for you in the car? I can manage these if you need to go."

"No. She's gone with a guy called Stephen. One of your class, I think. They danced together a couple of times. I'm pleased for her if she's making a new friend, so I told her to go. Perhaps you and I can find somewhere for a drink? Maybe something to eat?"

"Oh, I don't know. It's been a busy day."

"All the more reason to come with me and take a break. Please? There's something I'd like your opinion on."

"Alright," Annie said, puzzled now. She had met William several times, but she wasn't certain she really knew him at all. A long chat might be enlightening. She liked him a lot. She enjoyed his easy company, thoughtfulness and gentle manner.

"Yes, you're absolutely right. Somewhere quiet would be great," she said.

William carried her bag as he ushered her out of the door, and they walked side by side down the path and around to their cars. He placed her things on the back seat and opened her door for her. As he leaned in to suggest where they might go, Annie looked over his shoulder and saw a pale face at the window of the kitchen. It was Harry, standing and watching them.

"Sorry, I missed where you said," she said to William.

"What about the Oak Tree? You know, the pub near the showground. I know it's only a chain place, but it'll be a bit quieter than somewhere in town."

"Perfect. I'll see you there." Annie swivelled to catch her seatbelt and pull it across as William closed her door and walked away to his own car. When she looked at the kitchen window, it was empty. She sat for a second, pondering whether to go and knock on the door. Then she drew in a deep breath, confused by the events of the late afternoon. Looking again at the empty window, she decided against it and turned her car to follow William.

As she drove, there was so much to think about. She wanted to analyse how well the dance had gone, but she put that to one side for a moment. She needed to think about Harry. She pondered how and when he'd learned to dance. He had professed to have two left feet not long ago, and he had certainly smartened himself up. He had kissed her, albeit fleetingly. His lips were soft and warm, and dry. Sensual. But recently he had told her he had feelings for another lady.

Oh, Annie. You're letting your imagination run away with you. It's your own emotions getting you confused. As you danced, you were transported back to the school disco, that's all. Since she was about to have a pleasant evening with William, she decided to let Harry get on with his life. She would enjoy his simple companionship when it was offered, and she'd ask for no more.

Sitting down opposite William at the pub, Annie picked up the lemon and lime he had thoughtfully bought for her and took a large gulp. It burned her throat, but she needed the refreshment, and she was grateful to him.

"What would you like to eat?"

With food and drinks organised, Annie waited patiently for William to start the conversation proper and tell her what was on his mind. At the end of the dance, he'd hinted that he wanted her opinion, but he seemed to be finding it tricky to get to the point. If he was going to tell her he no longer wished to see her, this was not the way to do it, surely, over dinner. If that was it, she would be disappointed, she realised, but her world would not be shattered either. Still, he was someone who would be an exceptionally good friend, so she'd be sorry not to see him again.

In the end, it was Annie who kickstarted the conversation. "So, William, what is it you wanted to talk to me about?"

"It's awkward." He looked down and readjusted the serviette on his lap.

"If you want to tell me you don't want to see me again…" Annie would make it easy for the poor man.

"Oh no, nothing like that. Well… It's… I don't know. The thing is…" William sighed. "The thing is, I don't know what I want. I never have."

"What do you mean, never?"

"My father was in the army. We travelled quite a bit and then settled in Aldershot. He was a captain by the time he retired. A professional rank that most will get to, no high-flyer, but he loved the life. All that macho marching around and men's company. He was strict with me, and he hoped I'd follow in his footsteps, I think."

"But you didn't."

"No way. That life wasn't for me at all. I hated sport. I didn't enjoy the Scouts. I liked reading. I wasn't an ace at anything at school, really. I've been a complete disappointment to him."

"What about your mum?"

"She's always stood up for me, but it's hard for her. He's such a strong character. She was over the moon when I got married and we had Natalie. She's adopted, actually. Mum wasn't surprised it all went wrong, though. She told me she'd always thought I wasn't the marrying kind."

"What does that mean? You're thoughtful and kind. Lots of women like that. If you're sensitive, then life can be hard. I understand that much."

William took a large swig of his lager and said nothing for several moments, avoiding Annie's eyes. His face contorted. He frowned. His mouth twisted with concentration, and he took a deep breath.

"William, just say it. I won't be shocked or upset. Tell me what you're thinking." Annie leaned across the table and touched his hand with the tips of her fingers.

"I think my marriage was a huge mistake. I was trying to prove to my family and friends that I am like them, but I'm not. Same with all this Partner.com stuff."

"Like them … how?"

"Interested in women, all the stuff that goes with that. Oh, Annie, I think I'm … I'm asexual."

"Okay," Annie whispered as she played for time.

"I've read about it," William said, fiddling with his glass. "I am romantically attracted to people occasionally, but I get no pleasure or joy from the sex side of things. I'm sorry. This is embarrassing for you. I wanted to explain. It's not you who I don't find attractive or anything. You're wonderful. Lovely."

"Hush, it's fine, William. Do you think you might be gay?"

"No, I'm certain it's not that. I mean, I enjoy a hug and a kiss with a woman, but I don't have any desire to go further. I've never wanted to hug or kiss a man. I think my wife thought I was odd. She couldn't handle it. I mean, we're good friends now, but that's all. When I was at secondary school and all the lads were eyeing up the girls, I had no interest. You know at that age boys are into all sorts of stuff — magazines and suchlike — but I never was. I don't think it's going to change any time soon. I wanted to be fair to you."

"You're being very fair. William, you're a very dear man. I'd love to be your friend, you know."

"What, even if it's not going anywhere?"

"Of course. There's the cinema to share, times like now, a quiet meal. It's always truly good to have a man to share things with and to ask for opinions. Is that why you dived out to the toilets for the last waltz?" Annie chuckled. "Great avoidance strategy."

"Yes, it is. I didn't want to let you think I wanted that type of intimacy."

"You don't need to be fearful at all. I'm so pleased you've told me."

"Who was the guy you ended up dancing with?"

"Ah! That was Harry. Harry Moon. We were at school together."

"That makes sense. He looked like he was enjoying the dance. I wonder if, perhaps, he would like to be more than an old acquaintance."

"No. He's just a friend, too." Annie told William how she had bumped into Harry, literally, and how he'd helped her secure Moondreams House as the premises for her dance school. "He told me he has met a lady in whom he's very interested, so there's no chance there."

CHAPTER 24

Harry watched the other man lean towards Annie as she sat in her car. This must be the William of whom she'd talked. He seemed pleasant enough but unremarkable, from what he'd seen. Annie had said he was kind and thoughtful. Damn the man! Why did he have to be so nice? The sinking feeling in the pit of his stomach was so familiar. Perhaps he should try to forget Annie altogether and concentrate on other things. It was becoming more and more difficult to do that, though.

Annie was shielded from his sight as William leant into the car. As Harry watched, he could only imagine the kiss she might be receiving. He couldn't bear it. He'd so nearly made a complete fool of himself in the ballroom. The dance had been fine. He'd been pleased with himself, with his finesse in handling the steps. He'd remembered what David had told him and flexed his knees and used his toes. It had been smooth, and he'd felt the flow of the music. He'd also been overwhelmed by Annie being in his arms — her warmth, the rhythm of her movements as she'd danced, the perfume she wore. He'd dared to dream. When she'd looked up at him and whispered his name, he'd been unable to bring himself to speak. His voice would have cracked. He loved her to distraction. The tired old Harry was pared away. There, underneath, was the fresh, young man he used to be. He'd soared in that moment.

Then, when all was finished and he'd seen Annie with William, he'd realised what a fool he was to dream. Even if she had feelings for him — and she had shown no signs of that — she might want children. Harry couldn't risk that, not after what had happened all those years ago. He moved away from the window.

David appeared in the kitchen behind him, interrupting his thoughts. "The dance seemed to go well, don't you think? I admit I had my reservations, but it was good to see the room being used for its intended purpose. Perhaps I'll suggest to Annie that she organises another one soon."

Harry lifted his head. "Er ... yes. There were more people there than I thought there might be."

"Are you alright, man? You seem distracted."

"I'm fine. Shall I put the kettle on?"

"That's what I came to do. I even enjoyed the dance I had with that lady, Edith Hill. She seems a pleasant, uncomplicated person, and she dances well for a beginner."

Harry roused himself. "Do you know her well?"

"No. I met her the other week. Remember? I looked in on one of the classes, and Annie persuaded me to partner her because that young lad who she usually dances with hadn't appeared. I understand she likes him, but they were only thrown together because there wasn't an alternative. It's not a suitable arrangement, really." David was rarely so verbose.

"So ... you old goat. Did you go looking for her today?"

"Really, Harry!"

"You did, didn't you?"

"I used to enjoy dancing. That's all. Don't go making more of it than is there." David changed the subject. "I think we need to get the roof looked at. That brown stain is getting worse. Contact Heritage Roofing, would you? Ask them to come back and discuss it with me as soon as possible. We could end up with the ceiling all over the floor at this rate."

"I'll get onto it first thing tomorrow morning."

Well, this was a new turn. David, at last, seemed to have woken up to the state of the house.

"Let's hope nothing bad happens before it's fixed, Harry," he said. "That could put a stop to Annie's classes, never mind any future plans for dances."

"Now that the ballroom's in use, it would be even sadder to lose it." Harry could say nothing more.

Now back at home, Annie sat down and sighed. She'd enjoyed her first experience of organising and running a social dance. It was all highly invigorating and she was buzzing with ideas. So many of the people had come to her at the end and said they had enjoyed it. The programme she had put together catered for everyone's level of experience, and they'd liked the cakes. Hopefully, Sarah would get extra business from it, too.

The words of Ellie's friend, Liv, returned. Perhaps an evening event would be perfectly possible. Annie would need to talk to David, of course. Would she need to organise an outside bar? People could bring their own snacks and nibbles if they wished. She would decorate the tables. She could afford to do that now. There might be a theme. Perhaps red, white, and blue? This demanded some consideration.

Annie's thoughts turned to David. Fancy him coming and dancing with Edith! It was all very satisfying. As for her own last dance and that kiss with Harry... The strength of her emotions had surprised her. It had felt so … so right, somehow, yet he had another woman somewhere. He had told her.

In the meantime, she had classes to resume next week and needed to prepare.

Later that week, Ginny sat at the small table in Annie's kitchen, her hands around a steaming mug.

"Did Ellie enjoy serving at the dance? Do you think she'd do it again?" asked Annie.

"She was well made up, especially with what you paid her. Never mind that, though. Tell me how it's going with William."

"Hmm. He's a lovely, perceptive, sensitive man. We won't be taking it further than friendship, but we'll continue seeing each other." For some reason, Annie couldn't bring herself to share the conversation she'd had with him. It seemed disloyal. Nor did she tell of the dance and the kiss she'd had with Harry.

"He sounds a paragon. Why won't you be taking it further?" Ginny frowned. "It's early days to say that. Just wait and see."

"Sometimes you know there's not that sort of spark, but he'll be a good friend," Annie said. She hoped the tone she used would stop further questioning.

The conversation took a different turn. "Ellie said you didn't have the last dance with William." Ginny leaned forward with her head to one side and raised her eyebrows. "You did take part, though — I presume with Harry? So come on, fess up."

Annie sighed and smiled. "Nothing gets past you."

"Too right." Ginny laughed uproariously. "You know me. Tell all, then."

"There's really nothing to tell. William went off to the loo. There's a lady Harry fancies, apparently."

"Oh." Ginny looked peeved. "Who is she, then?"

"I have no idea. To me he's a friend, but he's not going to give me all the details of his private life. I'm pleased for him, though."

"Right. Like you are truly pleased."

"I am," Annie persisted. "Of course, I am."

"The lady doth protest too much, methinks! What are you going to do?"

"Nothing." Annie was self-conscious under Ginny's scrutiny. She couldn't deny she had sensed a great desire while Harry and she were dancing. That feeling just below her navel and the catch in her chest as he'd kissed her lightly were still vivid. The light in his eyes had shone as he'd looked down at her. Surely she hadn't misinterpreted that.

And then that kiss. The memory of it returned with fresh intensity. Had it been a kiss of friendship? Or something more?

CHAPTER 25

Annie took three telephone calls in quick succession. Two were from couples who had decided they ought to brush up some of their ballroom steps. They had both been doing sequence dances for a while but had enjoyed the social dance so much, they each wanted to be able to dance the straight sections with greater confidence. Annie thought on the spot and suggested they join her later group. The other call was even more of a surprise. It was from Natalie.

"I'd like to take up proper ballroom and Latin dancing rather than going back to the sequences we learned when I was with my dad," she said. "Do you have a space for me in the class that Stephen goes to?"

"I do, but you might find it tricky to catch up now," Annie replied. *Also, that gives me a problem with Edith*, she thought to herself.

"I know some of the steps from what we did before. I managed with guidance at the social dance. I'd really, really like to."

I wonder how much this has to do with Stephen? Annie thought.

She could support Edith for the moment, but it would be difficult to manage in the long term. She needed to be free to help all the students. After all, they were all paying the same fee. Perhaps she'd need to re-double her efforts to find an assistant. There was always Gillian. She had the expertise, and Annie liked her.

"I can tell you're not sure," Natalie went on. "I really hope you will take me."

Annie caved in. "Why don't you come for say, two weeks, and we'll see how it goes? If you find you can't keep up, I might be starting another beginners' class in the autumn."

"Oh, that's great. Thank you so much."

Annie put the phone down and sank onto a chair. This was wonderful in many ways, but it left her with quite a predicament. Then she had a flash of inspiration and made a phone call.

"Hi, William," Annie said with her fingers crossed. She explained the situation with Natalie and the complication of Edith. "So, I was wondering, well, hoping that you might consider coming, too."

"Ah, Annie," he began. Annie's shoulders sank. This was not going to be good. "The thing is … I have just joined a gardening group, and it's that same evening. Apart from that, though, I don't think I should come and cramp Natalie's style. She's making friends, and I suspect the last thing she needs is her dad watching."

"Yes, of course. You're absolutely right. Don't worry. I'll find another solution," Annie said. *Oh, heck!* she thought. *Now what?*

"Really sorry. Are we still on for that quiz night at the Salvation Army place? I do hope so."

"Yes, of course. I'm looking forward to it. And really, with the other thing, no worries." She said goodbye and rang off.

Annie considered her other options, but they were few. She could ask Harry. Perhaps if she phrased it as a favour he might do it, and he would get a free lesson.

The more Annie thought about it, the better the idea seemed. She decided to go for it and rang Harry before she changed her mind.

"Oh Lord, I don't know," he said when Annie explained her problem.

She decided he needed a push. "You'd be doing me a great favour. I'm in a bit of a fix with this one. And you'll get a free lesson. If you want to impress your lady friend, it might help."

There was a long pause and Annie fidgeted and bit her lip, determined not to be the first to speak.

Finally, Harry answered. "Alright. I'll give it a try."

Annie was fulsome in her thanks before she hung up.

Harry was waiting for her when she arrived for the early lesson. "I'm really not sure about this, Annie," he said.

"Don't say that." She gave him her best agonised look. "Let's give it a couple of weeks and see how it goes. Between us, I think Edith had a bit of a crush on Stephen, so this helps me out in more ways than one. He's been fine about it, but he needs someone his own age. Natalie would be perfect."

"Not matchmaking, are you?" Harry put his head on one side and grimaced. "Okay. If it helps you out of a hole. David told me he thought Edith was a lovely lady."

"Perhaps he'd take over," Annie suggested, but then it was her turn to pull a face. The thought of David in her lessons every week was very scary, so she added, "Although this class is a bit basic for him."

"Does this Edith know what's happening?"

"Yes, I rang and told her. She was happy about it because she wants to continue coming to learn." Annie forbore to tell Harry that she'd been extremely disappointed not to be dancing with Stephen.

"Oh dear," she'd said. "He and I get on so well. I … well … I understand." Annie had imagined Edith sitting up straight and pulling her shoulders back in her no-nonsense manner.

"He'll be looking for a partner nearer his own age." She'd gusted a sigh and Annie had been sorry for her. She'd been a lonely soul since her sister had departed.

The class arrived in their couples and Edith on her own. Stephen placed his hand on Natalie's back as he guided her through the door. So, they had come together. Annie glanced at Edith, who was watching with an expression of desolation. She signalled to Harry, who walked across to her. "Edith, this is Harry. He'll learn with you tonight."

Harry must have witnessed Edith's expression, appraised the situation and got it right because he said, "I'm so pleased you have agreed to be my partner this evening. I have a friend that I should like to impress with my dancing, and it needs to be better than it is."

"I'm glad to be of help, then," Edith said.

Crisis over, I hope, Annie thought and introduced the lesson. "Let's get warmed up with a cha-cha-cha. Don't forget, you get the hip movement by alternate bending and straightening of the knees. The weighted leg will be straight, and the free leg will bend. Oh, and don't forget to use the balls of your feet before you lower your heel. Watch first. Like this." Annie swayed to the beat in her head and then put on some music. She started to count to get them all going.

She got a genuine thrill from seeing this group making steady progress and gaining confidence. Morag's lips still moved as she counted, but not all the time these days. Annie couldn't help noticing Harry's neat backside in his well-cut trousers as he moved, but when the dance finished, she remembered to give praise where it was due, and she noted a beaming smile on Edith's face. James put his arm around Christine's shoulders, and she smiled up at him.

About a quarter of an hour before the end of the lesson the internal door opened, and David crept in. Edith noticed straight away. With a word to Harry, she scuttled towards him. Annie had no idea what was said, but he advanced with her into the room. He had a word with Harry, who retreated to the side and to Annie's amazement, David took his place.

The older man inclined his head to Annie and said, "May I?"

Annie looked across at Harry, who nodded.

The last dance was a run through of the waltz step, and Edith seemed to fit very snugly in David's arms as an instrumental version of 'Que Sera, Sera (Whatever Will be, Will Be)' wafted around the ballroom with the dancers.

At the end of the lesson, David approached Annie. "Mrs Ellis…"

"Annie," she said and smiled her encouragement.

"Annie … I hope you don't mind me hijacking your arrangement with Harry. He shared your predicament with me. I'd be happy to partner Edith for the next few weeks."

"Oh, David, that would be marvellous. Are you sure? It's quite basic work we're still doing."

"It would be my pleasure. I'm sure the practice would do me good. I'll ask Edith if that would be acceptable to her, shall I?"

"Please do," Annie said.

The smile on Edith's face was Annie's answer.

"I'm more than happy with that," Harry said, when Annie updated him.

"Why don't you ask your friend if she wants to come to the lessons, Harry? You would both be very welcome."

"We'll see," he answered. "I'll be back later, after your second class. They're starting to arrive." He nodded in the direction of the outside door as it opened. Annie turned to welcome the first of the new couples.

As the second lesson finished, Harry appeared again through the internal door. He was filled with a sense of anticipation but stood silently and watched as Annie said goodbye to her students. The new people told her they'd be back the following week.

"It's all starting to take off well," he said across the hall as the last ones left. "I'm so pleased for you."

"You're a dark horse," Annie said. "Where *have* you been learning to dance?"

"David showed me a step or two. You know we've been trying to involve him and perk up his interest in the whole place."

"Ah, yes. So that's it. Now he's going to partner Edith, so it appears to be working. Is he going to do anything about that?" She nodded at the ugly patch on the ceiling.

"It would seem that he is. Annie … moving on … would you show me a step I'm stuck with? I can't seem to get the footwork right."

"Okay. What is it?"

"A closed impetus? I think it's called that."

"Ah, yes. It has a heel turn for the man, which you may not have come across before. Ladies do heel turns quite a lot, especially in the foxtrot."

"Crikey! I'm not that far in yet." Harry smiled.

"Come here and I'll show you. Go back on your left foot and as the right foot closes, that's when you do the heel turn. Then you place your left foot to the side and slightly back. If you come to me in hold, I'll do my steps and count us through it."

As Harry took her in his arms, he was breathless and his heart started thumping.

"Try and relax. You seem tense."

Yes, he was. This had seemed like a good idea at the time, but now…

"Shall I put some music on and we'll see how you lead into it, so it becomes part of your routine?"

Annie put on an instrumental version of Seal's 'Kiss from a Rose' and walked towards him as the introduction played. She brought her arms up and Harry put his hand on her shoulder blade, taking her right hand in his left.

"Elbows up and stand close. We'll start with some basics, then a couple of turns, natural and a reverse, then the other stuff, including the closed impetus. Is that okay?"

Harry nodded and Annie counted them in.

He was lost. The feel of her slender hips against his and the smell of her perfume were tantalising. He took a deep breath to calm himself.

When the last notes resonated, he couldn't release her. He needed to kiss her. But if he did, he wouldn't want to stop. His heart beat even faster. She looked up at him, and her face lost focus. In that moment, he bent his head as her lips came towards his. The kiss they shared was deep, not fleeting like the last. She was responding.

"Oh, Annie," he whispered. "It's you. There's never been anyone like this. Ever. It's only ever been you." He leaned to kiss her again and took the back of her head in his hand. His other hand caressed her face and his thumb grazed her cheek. He was aware of her lips parting and dared to risk the tip of his tongue against hers. Annie groaned almost imperceptibly.

In a panic, Harry pulled away. "I'm sorry," he said. "I can't. I *must* not."

With that, he turned and without looking back, he strode away from her.

CHAPTER 26

Annie stood still and watched Harry leave. Her knees were trembling. She was stunned. He'd said it had always been her, but then he'd stopped himself. What was that about? Why? She was sorely tempted to run after him. She took a step and raised her arm at his retreating back, but she couldn't find her voice. She needed to think. She staggered back to the table where her things were and collapsed onto a chair. After feeling a surging tide of warmth, she was now left dizzy and empty like a piece of flotsam tossed randomly and washed up on a deserted shore.

Annie wasn't transported back to her school days this time. She was here, right in the moment. Harry's arms, Harry's lips on hers, the rasp of his chin. She touched her own, where the sensation of him still tingled. Harry, always kind and considerate. Harry, totally aware of others and especially her. Why hadn't she realised all of this sooner? She'd been so wrapped up in her search for a companion. First the arrogant Nigel, then William, who was becoming a good friend but would never be anything more. And now Harry. Yet he'd said he'd met a lady. Was that her? Confused thoughts ran wildly through her mind.

Annie bundled her things together and prepared to go home. She needed space to think this through. She realised she was nervous, but full of anticipation.

The weather outside was changing and the door resisted her push because the wind was getting up. A drizzle had started, and the sky was darkening. The trees behind the lawn thrashed. With her head down, Annie scuttled along the path, thrust everything into her boot and, slamming it shut, she hurried into her car. With her arms folded tight across her chest, her shoulders hunched and her hands tucked in, she sought comfort and warmth. She looked across to the window of the kitchen, but it only reflected the flat, grey sky.

By the time she was home, the rain was heavy. Fat globules of water bounced off the bonnet of her car and hit the windscreen. She grabbed her handbag but left all her other things to collect later and careered along the short path to the front door. A towel for her hair, her pyjamas and her dressing gown were what she needed. She gave Raffa a quick stroke, opened the dog flap for him and plodded upstairs. She would shower in the morning. Her energy had dissipated, but she would try to make sense of her emotions before going to bed.

A loud crack woke Annie up in the early hours. As she lay, momentarily disorientated, there was a flash and, with the instinct from childhood, she started to count, only reaching five before the next crash resounded. After such a long dry spell, this storm was the natural result. She had never been completely happy with such weather since a house opposite her parents' home had been struck by lightning, and she knew Raffa would be restless.

As she bent to stroke his ears down in the kitchen, there was another flash of lightning, although this time the thunder had moved away a little. "A cup of tea, I think. Would you like a special treat?" Annie found Raffa a biscuit and sat at the table, waiting for the kettle to boil. "I'm going to ring Harry in the morning," she said to the little dog. "I'll say we should meet and talk. I need to tell him I love him, too." *I didn't realise before, but now I do. I'm sure of it.* It was different from what she'd felt for Rob, but it was just as intense.

Annie looked across at the picture of her and Rob on their last holiday. *Thank you for the years we had, for everything you gave me and did for me*, she thought. *Thank you for letting me move on, at last. I'll always love you, you must know that, but this is different. This is me being an equal partner. I didn't need that with you but now I do. I've changed because I've had to. I need something distinct, for me, and someone to support that. Someone who needs me, too.* Tears crept into the corners of her eyes, but they weren't tears of sadness. She was yearning to be with Harry; to have his arms around her again and to share all these thoughts with him.

Annie settled Rafferty back down and took her tea upstairs. She lay for some time, reliving the moment of dawning realisation following the extraordinary experience of Harry's kiss. Then she snuggled down and with a wide smile still on her face, and thoughts of talking with Harry in the morning, she fell asleep again.

The buzzing was insistent. Annie was enjoying the sound of a large bee following the scent of the flowers around the lawn at Moondreams House as she lay with someone on a rug. She couldn't see that person's face, but his arms were comforting, and the sun was warm on her eyelids as she lay dozing. She came awake gradually and the buzzing continued. Someone was calling.

She sat up and grabbed her phone. Was this Harry? As she answered, she glanced at the grey day outside, through a crack in the curtains.

"Annie, good morning."

Annie was taken aback. "Hello?" Who was this?

"I'm so sorry to telephone you early, before it's even nine o'clock."

Annie glanced at the clock. It was eight-fifty. "Is that David?"

"Yes. There's been a bit of a … well … an incident."

Her heart skipped. "Is everybody alright?"

"Yes, oh yes. No one is hurt. I wondered if you could come over. Better to have a chat face to face."

"Right. I could be with you in about half an hour. Can you give me a clue? Is Harry there?"

"Er … good. I'll see you soon then. About half an hour. Thank you." The line was disconnected.

Annie's sense of foreboding grew as she threw on jeans and a T-shirt. Why had David sounded so cryptic? Then in the next breath she decided it was not in his nature to be verbose. When had he ever used six words when two would do? It was probably nothing much. Maybe he wanted to discuss details of the next dance. But he could do that at the end of next week's lessons.

Her thoughts bounced back and forth as she drove to Moondreams House. When she realised her speed had increased, she made a concerted effort to concentrate and keep within safer limits on the winding roads. The last thing she needed was to meet an unexpected tractor head-on. After the rain, the roads were probably slippery.

As she parked in her now habitual spot, she couldn't resist a glance at the kitchen window, but nobody was looking out. Of course, Harry didn't know that she desperately wanted to talk to him. She would see what David needed so urgently and, although she would be stamping with frustration, she would listen until she could ask to see Harry.

Annie opened the kitchen door and called out. "Hello! David?" There was no answer, but the house was large and if he was upstairs, she'd have to go into the cavernous front

176

entrance hall to be heard. She crossed the kitchen and shouted again.

A door slammed and footsteps sounded. Eventually David appeared. "Ah, Annie, so good of you to come." He held out both hands to her. This was uncharacteristic of the man she had come to know. She took his hands, and he drew her along the passageway and the hall beyond.

As he stood on the faded rug, he turned to her. "We have a bit of a catastrophe."

Annie's heart started to race. "What on earth is it? You said everyone was fine."

"You better come and look." David led the way to the ballroom, and Annie started to have an inkling of what might have happened. Perhaps the water stain was worse, and he would need to get the people in to fix it sooner than he'd thought.

As they approached, there was an odour of decay. Dead rats sprang to Annie's mind. She put the back of her hand to her nose to mask the stench. It was strong and musty and awful.

David pushed the door open and Annie gasped. The sight she beheld drove all else from her mind. She didn't know what to say. "Oh, David," was all she could summon at first. As she became accustomed to the dreadful odour, her hand moved from her nose to her mouth. Half of the ceiling was lying on the beautiful dancefloor.

"It's all my fault," David said and hung his head. "I should have listened. Harry's been on at me for months, well, probably years."

"The brown stain has been getting worse." Annie grimaced but refrained from further criticism.

"I've left a message on the answerphone for Heritage Roofing. They're down to come and do some work on the roof in a couple of weeks, but it'll need rather more work now than the original quote was for. We need a whole new ceiling as well as the external work."

"Oh dear. I see why you needed me to come, now."

"I couldn't have started to describe this or how I feel about it. There's an awful lot of cleaning up to be done. Mrs M and I can make a start on it later, but the smell is terrible, isn't it?"

"It is fairly appalling." Annie smiled at him to try and remove the sting of her honesty. "I'm happy to come and help."

"I'm so sorry, my dear. I am totally responsible."

Annie laid her hand on his arm. "We need to get the rubbish cleared away. I imagine that would save a tiny amount on the bill. It might help the smell, too. Anyway, we need to protect the floor as much as possible, and we can't do that with all this everywhere."

"I really don't think you could run your classes in here for a while, even if we clear up the floor."

"No. I don't think it would be healthy." Annie's heart sank, and her cheeks puffed out. "Right! I need to go home and change. With all four of us — Mrs M, you, me, and Harry — we'll get this cleared up. I'll need to think of something for my dance classes, though." Annie sighed. She knew how much other local places would cost, and this had been so perfect.

"I've been thinking about that, since this is all my responsibility."

Annie looked at David in surprise.

"I wondered if you could manage with the entrance hall. It's only half the size of this room, of course, but we could roll up the Turkey rug. The floor underneath is in good condition. It's made from early Victorian tiles rather than wood, but we had it all restored, cleaned, and sealed some years ago. It was the last thing Jane oversaw before she passed away."

"I didn't notice the floor. I only looked at the carpet in there, which is amazing."

"Let's go through that way." David indicated she should precede him. "Come and have a look and let me know what you think. Of course, there will no charge until we get the ballroom back into working order."

Annie's cheeks puffed out once more as she thought about the suggestion. "Well, yes. I think we could manage here," she said as they returned to the entrance hall.

David pulled back the corner of the large rug to reveal an immaculate geometric pattern in shades of terracotta, blue and small amounts of old gold and white.

"We re-laid the rug to protect the tiles, but a little dancing won't hurt," he said as he replaced the corner. "It's stiletto heels that would do the damage."

"It's beautiful. I think the noise would drift up to you, though. I'm aware that we mustn't disturb you. Students would have to come through the front door or else through the kitchen and along the passageway. I think you'd hear the music, too."

"My dear, if I'm in the class to help Edith, it wouldn't disturb me, would it?"

"Er … um … no, it wouldn't." Annie was lost for words again and looked sideways at him, but he studiously avoided her gaze. "Okay," she said at length. "Well, I better go and get changed. Might I have a word with Harry first? Is he around?"

"Normally I wouldn't even consider you helping with such a messy task, but I must say I would be grateful. I'm not good at being energetic at my age, and Mrs M won't be up for much, although her husband might agree to come and help. The thing is, Harry's not here."

"Oh. When will he be back? Will he be long, do you think?" Annie guessed he'd gone shopping for cleaning equipment.

"He's going to be gone for a while. He came to me last night and asked to take a holiday. Since he's not had one for years, probably, I said he certainly could. Actually, he seemed a little distressed about something. I must admit I was surprised when he took off straight away, in all that awful weather. It was before all this lot happened, of course."

"Last night? It must have been late. Where's he gone?" Annie's stomach churned. She was chilly all of a sudden.

"I really have no idea, I'm afraid. I didn't ask, and he went so hurriedly."

"Oh," she said bleakly. A rush of helplessness took her breath. "Right. Um … well, I better go and get sorted. I'll be back soon."

Annie nursed her mug as she sat hunched at Ginny's kitchen table.

"The thing is, I can't help but think it's related to what happened yesterday evening. It's got to be. Why else would he suddenly take off like he has? He said he *must* not, after we kissed. I assumed he meant that he mustn't allow himself to fall in love again. Something's gone on, Ginny — in the past, I mean — but I can't imagine what. It must be more than his failed marriage. That was years ago, and he's picked himself up completely. Well, so I thought. And where's he gone, for goodness' sake? David said he seemed distressed about something."

"Calm down. You're talking nineteen to the dozen. You need to go and give David a hand, by the sound of things, so your classes can run. Apart from anything else, it'll take your mind off this disappearance. Harry will be back. You'll see. Give him time to sort out his emotions. I'll come over later and give a hand, if you like."

"Ginny, would you? That would be such a help. David's quite ancient for this sort of work, and I suspect Mrs M won't be much help. David said he'd see if her husband would come, but I think he's working on a building site somewhere. I better get along. Sitting here won't get anything done. You're probably right about Harry. I'm putting too much on it all."

"I'm not saying I'm up to much. I'm not the right shape for manual work, but I'll give it a shot. As for the Harry thing, wait a couple of days. I'm sure he'll be back sooner than you think. Look, I've got to nip to the supermarket, so I'll meet you at the house later."

"You're a truly remarkable friend, Ginny. Thank you."

As Annie changed into some old painting clothes, she racked her brain to try and understand why Harry had taken off in such a rush. Maybe Ginny was correct, and it was nothing to do with what had happened and she was making a mountain out of a molehill. After all, she wasn't really that important to him, was she? But he'd said it had *always* been her. His kisses were real, and they were significant. Annie was certain of it as she relived the feel of him as he'd held her. The tenderness and longing had been tangible, honest, and fervent. Surely she hadn't invented that.

She now realised that the thing she'd been craving had been in front of her the whole time. How ridiculous she had been, to go through all the angst of using Partner. Maybe she had needed to go through that, though, to understand what she really desired.

CHAPTER 27

Back at Moondreams House, David held out a piece of fabric to Annie. "Here, take one of these. It may help with the smell a little, and anyway, it's very dusty."

"Facemasks. That's a good idea. Where did you get these?"

"I had them when Jane was ill. I tried every little thing to prevent her getting infections that would bring the end closer. The doctor gave us a stock. They've been lying wrapped up in a drawer since then."

"Ah!"

"Well, go on. Put it on." David showed a spark of the defensive man he had become since Jane's death, but he didn't frighten Annie anymore.

She had tied an old scarf over her hair, and she managed to pull the elastic of the mask around her ears. Turning to practicalities, she said, "Have you a wheelbarrow? We could pile all the stuff in one. It would be quicker to remove than carrying it. Where shall we dump it all?"

"There's space at the back of the old kitchen garden, around the corner. I'll fetch the barrow. I wasn't able to contact Mrs M, but I found these old dustsheets to cover the rest of the floor."

"Do you think it's safe to stand under the bit of ceiling that's still up there?" Annie glanced up.

"The men from Heritage Roofing came while you were gone. They said it was alright, and they also said they can rejig their schedule and come a week earlier." David disappeared into the garden.

He's stepping up, Annie thought. *He certainly wasn't this engaged with anything when I first met him. With Harry gone, I suppose he's had to take control.*

When David reappeared, pushing an ancient and heavy-looking wheelbarrow, Annie told him Ginny would be coming later. He expressed his gratitude. "It's still going to be hard work, so please do stop when you need to."

They set at it, trying to gather the jumbled chunks of plaster, laths and copious amounts of dust and filth. Cobwebs laced with years of grime covered much of it like a thin fabric. They had been working for half an hour when there was the sound of a car approaching. Annie looked up, and her heart started to beat harder. Could this be Harry returning already?

As she picked her way through the muck, she glanced at the footpath that led to the door. What she saw surprised and warmed her, even though it wasn't Harry. It was James, Cameron, Ted, Mick and Stephen. They all stood in work clothes, and each carried gloves of various kinds. James had a shovel in his hand and Ted carried an assortment of cleaning products. Tears leaked from the corners of Annie's eyes, both from disappointment that it wasn't Harry and extreme gratitude to these lovely men.

She turned to David and explained that she had called James to say that the class would run in the smaller entrance hall. "I was going to talk to the others, too, but James said he'd start the ball rolling with everyone else."

The men made their way to the ballroom.

"My Lord, that's boggin', right enough," said Cameron. He put his hand to his nose.

"We've come to lend a hand," Stephen said. "James rang all of us after you let him know."

"Guys, we are so, so grateful," Annie said as she handed them facemasks.

David echoed her sentiment.

They had got a lot cleared away by the time Ginny arrived. Annie was so busy she'd forgotten her friend was coming and hadn't let her know they had plenty of help.

"I'll make the coffee, shall I? I think that might be more my cup of tea." She laughed at her own little joke.

They all followed David to the kitchen and collapsed onto chairs around the table. Ginny poked about in the cupboards to find mugs. She had brought a large, round tin with her, and inside was an enormous three-layered chocolate cake with icing slathered on the top.

"Would you look at that," Cameron said. "Just as well our Gillian's not here to watch me eat it."

"This is so very kind of you all," David said. "I feel humbled, I truly do. Who knew the world could be so kind and decent? I'd forgotten, I admit." He stood and busied himself with fetching a cake knife and some plates, and Annie guessed it was to cover his emotions. What a changed man he was becoming.

Between them, they finished the job. After the others had left, David and Annie sat opposite each other at the kitchen table. "You have a very grubby face, young lady," he said and smiled at her with gentle eyes. "I really cannot thank you sufficiently."

Annie could not have imagined him like this a few short months ago. She pulled off her scarf and used it to wipe her cheeks. Her shoulders ached and she looked forward to a long, hot soak in the bath, probably with a glass of wine on the side. Before she left, though, she needed David's help.

"David, where do you think Harry might have gone? Have you any idea at all?"

"Did something happen last night? He did seem … discomposed. I might even say, well … tormented wouldn't be too strong. My dear, may I speak openly?"

"Please do."

"I know that things have been difficult for Harry. We both lost our way in this enormous place. For me, it was when I lost Jane. It's been like a mausoleum." He hung his head for several seconds before resuming eye contact. "I think Harry came to escape something. Well, he must speak for himself."

"I know his marriage failed, but that was years ago."

"Yes, it was," David said, "but there was something else, too. It frightened him, and he hasn't been able to forgive himself."

"Can't you tell me?"

"No, my dear. It's not my story to tell, but I think I know where he might be."

Annie leaned forward. Every nerve in her body was vibrating with a mixture of fear and anticipation.

"I'll give you the telephone number for his sister in Cornwall. I'm sure she won't mind. Speak to her. If I'm correct, she'll be able to tell you where he is. It's where he went all those years back. His bolthole. Ultimately, family support each other. Find him and ask him about the past. I'm sure he'll tell you, of all people, and you'll be able to help each other."

Back at home, Annie rang the telephone number David had given her.

"Hello, Lucy Moon speaking," said a disjointed voice.

"I'm sorry to disturb you. You must be Harry's sister. My name is Annie Ellis."

"Ah, I'm pleased you've rung… Harry's not here right now."

Annie's heart descended and her shoulders slumped. However, she registered that the woman at the other end of the line seemed to know about her.

"He often takes himself down to the sea front. He should be back soon," Lucy went on.

"Oh. Oh, I see." Annie closed her eyes and breathed in again.

After they spoke for a few minutes, Annie was no wiser about the circumstances. Lucy had said it would be a good idea for her to come to her house in Cornwall, if at all possible. "This isn't something to be discussed on the phone," she said. "I'm not prepared to tell you myself, but Harry should. He's built it up over the years until it's become almost all-consuming. I've tried to talk to him about it, but he refused to discuss it. Now, I'm guessing that his involvement with you, Annie, has brought it all back. He's become even more obsessed with the past. I appreciate that Cornwall is a long way from you, but you are welcome to stay with me for a couple of days, if that helps. I think Harry needs you, to be honest."

Having arranged practicalities, Annie said, "I'll ring again when I'm almost with you, if I may."

"Good idea. I won't tell that brother of mine you're coming. It's better that way." Lucy sounded sensible and grounded. "It's time this was sorted. He has never listened to me, even though I've tried to talk sense into him from time to time. We're not that close, I suppose, although he comes here when he's desperate." She chuckled. "Families, eh?"

Annie had already warmed to her.

Next, she needed to phone Si to ask if he'd look after Raffa for two or three days.

"Okay," Si said after Annie had made her request. "He'll be fine with me, but why on earth do you need to go all the way to Cornwall? That's a long journey for such a short time."

Annie couldn't bring herself to tell him all the details. "I have a friend in need. I said I'd go and talk to him."

"Him! Is it that Harry guy? I knew there was more to it than you let on. I remember I said at the beginning: don't go taking on a lame duck. But from the little you've said since, I gather he's not a layabout. You always were a loyal friend to people."

"Thank you, Si. I really appreciate it. I'll drop Raffa off on my way out in the morning and leave all his paraphernalia on the table."

CHAPTER 28

Harry took comfort from watching the sea churning. It reflected his mood, and the sound of the waves breaking was soothing, too. He wandered along the seafront until he came to a spot opposite the rocks. The swimming pool wall rose above, pale and flat. It had been painted again, probably at the beginning of the year for the new summer season, he thought vaguely. He stood and leaned on the railings. The wind blew his hair off his face. Perhaps it would also blow away this shroud of despair that was making his shoulders sag.

Annie had re-entered his life, and her presence had persuaded him that he was ready to consider the possibility of moving forward. Then he had delayed and dithered, and now he thought he'd lost her forever.

The kiss they had shared had reignited hope and desire in his heart, but then he had taken fright and panicked. Since then, he had hardly slept. His thoughts kept revolving around the same point: what if Annie wanted a child?

He couldn't go down that route again.

Harry's head sank into his hands as his elbows rested on the railings. He worked to calm his raging thoughts, but it was impossible. When he raised his head, his fingers were wet. He looked up at the grey sky and blinked away his tears as he watched a lone seagull battling against the stiff breeze. His ex-wife seemed to have been able to move on. She would never forget their child, she said, but she had found happiness again. But then, she hadn't been the one who'd caused the disaster, had she?

Annie had slept well, despite her disquiet. What on earth had Harry done — or thought he'd done, more likely? She couldn't stop thinking of his failed marriage. Perhaps he had caused money problems. Had he taken up gambling? Maybe it had been an accident of some kind, where someone had been injured. She hoped it wasn't an alcohol-related problem.

It would take her at least five or six hours to get to Penzance. She dropped Raffa at Si's house, stroked his ears, and got on the road.

About halfway, she stopped at a café and telephoned Lucy Moon to say she would be there just after lunch.

"No problem," Lucy said. "I've taken the day off work, so I'll be here. You must have made good time or left at the crack of dawn." Annie sensed a smile in her voice. "I'll have the kettle on for when you arrive, and then I'll tactfully disappear."

"I don't want to put you out," Annie said.

"It's no bother at all. I have stuff at the bowls club to see to anyway."

"Thank you. It's so kind of you. I'll see you soon." Annie rang off and left the café, uneasy about the next steps.

Conscious of driving carefully when her mind was elsewhere, Annie was nevertheless early, so she made a slight detour just after Crowlas and headed to Marazion. Here she pulled up in the car park near the Godolphin Hotel with a view along the slipway to St Michael's Mount, a tiny tidal island. Not only was she a little too early to find Lucy's house, she needed to try and eat something, though that would be hard. The nearer she got, the more nervous she was becoming.

Memories of the childhood holidays she'd spent here crowded her mind as she surveyed Mount's Bay, where the island lay. Many times, they had crossed the footpath, just before the tide had receded. It was much more fun to paddle across with cool waves lapping at her ankles, her hand secure in the warm grasp of her dad. Once over there, Annie had sat on the cobbles overlooking the tiny harbour with ice-cream dripping down her hands. Sometimes she had played ball games on the short, spiky grass where older folk had sat at the picnic tables below the castle. It was a special place to her.

Annie went looking for the pasty shop. She couldn't believe her luck when she found the shop still where it had been back in the day. She ate her pasty while perched on the low wall in front of her car. The air was tinged with seaweed. With the sun warm on her face, some of the tension eased from the back of her neck and shoulders.

She arrived in Penzance at the end of the lunchtime rush. Lucy's small, white bungalow overlooked the bay, and Annie pulled up alongside the kerb.

She took a deep breath. This was it. She was suddenly even more apprehensive. What if Harry thought she was meddling? Worse, what if she had come all this way and he was angry because she had cornered him? Casting a glance in the rear-view mirror, Annie dragged her fingers through her hair and pasted on a quick smear of lipstick before climbing out of the car.

She walked down the steep driveway past a garden with two small palm trees. Across the gable end of the bungalow, she found the front door through a gate at the side of the house. She knocked and stood back. Her knees were shaking, and her heart beat faster. Harry might open the door, and if she saw shock or anger on his face, she wouldn't know what to say. She wondered if this was a big mistake.

To Annie's relief, it was Lucy who answered the door. "Hello. You must be Annie. I'm pleased to meet you." She stuck out her hand.

Annie took it. "I'm pleased to be here," she said. "I think," she added and grimaced.

"No, it's good that you're here. I hope your journey hasn't been too difficult. It's such a long way. Come in, come in." Lucy stood back and Annie tentatively stepped inside the hallway. "My brother has gone into town, but he'll be back soon. I sent him out to get some milk. I thought it might be best if he was out when you arrived." She smiled with encouragement. "Then when he returns, I can say that we have a visitor before I leave you to it." She grinned.

"You've thought this through."

"Honestly, yes, I have. I'm so pleased you're here. Harry has come here in his hour of need, as it were, but he doesn't really listen to my opinion." Lucy shrugged. "It's a brother and younger sister thing, I guess. Just the way it is. Now come through and I'll put the kettle on. The bathroom is through there if you need it."

Annie beat a grateful retreat to the toilet. While she washed her hands, she had a swift look in the mirror and took the opportunity to comb her hair properly to calm her nerves.

They sat in a small, pleasant sitting room that overlooked the sea. Little waves and ripples sparkled in the afternoon sun, the wind and grey skies of earlier having departed. Annie nursed her mug of tea and was able to observe Harry's sister. She was small and sturdy, unlike her brother who was so tall. Her short hair shone, and her clothes were no-nonsense practical, but she had the same dark lashes framing bright blue Gaelic blue eyes that caught the light and twinkled like the sea behind her. Annie and Lucy spoke of generalities, carefully keeping away from the main reason for Annie's visit.

"Bring your bag in later, and I'll show you your room then," said Lucy. "I'm a committee member for the Bowls Club at the bottom of Lidden Road. I said I'd go and do some sorting out in the club house."

This little woman had warmth and fun about her, and Annie decided she would be just the person to come to in a crisis for that same warmth and down-to-earth good sense and understanding she was exuding.

"It's so good of you to…" Annie stopped mid-sentence as she heard a key in the front door and looked across at her hostess.

Lucy held up the flat of her hand to Annie, indicating that she should stay where she was. She then leapt up and went out into the hallway. "Harry, we have a visitor," Annie heard her say. Lucy spoke quietly, preventing Harry from entering until she had broken the news of who it was.

Annie put her mug down and stood. She wiped her hands down the sides of her trousers as the door to the sitting room was pushed wider and Harry came in.

His expression lit up when he saw her, but then his face went blank again. With a frown, he took a step back. "Annie. What are you doing here?"

Lucy had left them to talk. Harry paced the sitting room, sat down, and then stood again. When he suggested a walk, Annie was only too pleased.

They came out of the little bungalow and turned right, making their way to a narrow, sheltered footpath. Harry had his hands in his pockets and Annie's arms were folded. They could not have been more distant, although they had to walk close together down the footpath. Rich flora covered the high stone walls on each side and stunted trees had sprouted long ago from the tops. "It's called a Cornish hedge, despite the base being a wide-bottomed wall," Harry said, nodding at the mounds to their sides. "It's supposed to be really strong and a good windbreak. You find them all over the county."

"I'd have expected the tree roots to damage it," Annie said.

"I was reading up on it. There's a cycle of maintenance for just that reason."

Annie stopped walking. "Oh, for goodness' sake, Harry. I haven't come all this way to talk to you about the history of Cornish hedges."

"I know. I'm sorry," he said.

"Talk to me, then. Tell me all about whatever it is that's troubling you. We can work it out together, I'm sure. I need to tell you stuff too."

"Can we just walk for a while? I will tell you what I can. I will." Harry had stopped when she did and looked at her. Annie could see the worry in his eyes before he looked at his feet. "If we carry on along here, it joins Love Lane, and that'll take us down to the boating lake. We can sit on a bench and we'll talk there. I promise."

They walked in silence for several minutes. The day was one to be admired, but Annie could see, smell, and hear nothing but Harry by her side. He was much taller than her, which made her aware of his physical strength. She got exciting lemony whiffs of aftershave every now and then, and the sound of her own heart thumping masked any birdsong she might have heard. The sun hardly penetrated into the path but caught the tops of the foliage on the hedges. If Annie had had the heart to look, she'd have seen cow parsley, stitchwort and buttercups flowering in abundance and attracting insects.

By the time they had continued into Love Lane, the road was only a little wider. The sound of bicycle bells and a noisy hooter resounded close behind them. Annie, lost in thought, jumped and gasped. Harry pulled her to him as children on bikes sped past down the sloping lane. "Hey, steady," he called after them as his arms came around her.

He held her away, his hands still on her shoulders, hot and firm. "Are you okay? Thoughtlessness of youth, that's all."

Annie looked up at him, bit her bottom lip and nodded, unable to say anything.

Some of the earlier awkwardness had left Harry. He took her hand and led her to the end of Love Lane. They then turned left into Lariggan Road, and it wasn't long before they'd reached the cast-iron gates of the park. In the oblong boating lake, there were more water lilies and weeds than little boats. Harry led Annie to some benches in the shade of large laurel bushes on the far side. As they sat, he leaned forwards, his hands clasped between his knees.

Annie placed her hand on his shoulder and bent towards him, inhaling his scent. She could see his knuckles were white. "Harry," she whispered. "Share what happened with me."

CHAPTER 29

Annie's hand on his shoulder was a comfort. Somewhere in the back of his mind, Harry heard her whisper his name. His hands relaxed, but only for a moment.

He took a deep breath and plunged. "I was married once. I think you know that. I was young."

"You were with her after school. Just after our dance — or were you seeing her before we finished there? Did you know her at school?"

"No. We met very soon after, though. A bit of a rebound, I think, now."

"A rebound?"

"Yes. I thought our dance at that disco might've led somewhere. I'd fancied you for so long. But it ended before it began. I got teased about it. It was always tricky at school, wasn't it?" He shrugged and took a deep breath.

"Harry! If only I'd known. You were so popular. All the girls liked you. I guessed that dance was a one-off. I mean, why would you choose me when you could have had your pick?"

"I was lacking courage to talk to you, even then. The wisdom of the young, eh? I should have shrugged off the remarks from the other lads. I vaguely thought I'd ask you out once we'd finished school." Harry stared ahead and gathered his thoughts. "Anyway, Sheila and me. I met her straight after school. Too young, as I say, but a couple of friends were settling down. One got engaged. Another was going abroad. I was getting left behind. Sheila and I were together for a couple of years, and then she got pregnant. She was keen to get married." He shook his head and sat in silence while he remembered.

Annie cleared her throat, and he came back to the present. He glanced fleetingly at her but was too uncomfortable to make eye contact.

"She was determined to keep the baby. I mean, that was a good thing. We talked about waiting to get married. It wasn't like it used to be for our parents, but as I say, she was keen on it. Her mum was ecstatic and started planning everything. I went along with it. We managed to rent a small flat and the baby came along. I was happy enough at first. Got swept up in it all, I suppose."

"Tell me about the child."

"She was born perfect. I didn't have a clue, but we managed. Her mum came round a lot. That was a struggle for me, but Sheila was okay with it and she recovered. We were both completely knackered most of the time, but things seemed to be going alright. The baby slept, ate and did all the things tiny babies do, as far as I know." He smiled without mirth.

"So, what happened? I gather you no longer see the child. What did you call her? Does she live with Sheila?"

"She died." His voice sounded harsh, even to himself. There, the brutal truth was out — well, almost. He'd got this far. He would have to tell her the rest. He'd have to say the words. "I killed her. It was all my fault."

Harry heard a tiny intake of breath beside him, but Annie had the sense to say nothing. Her arm crept around his shoulders.

She'll remove that when I tell her how and why, Harry thought. He needed to stand and stretch and move about. It would save Annie the embarrassment of not knowing how to move away from him, too.

He stood with his back to her and said nothing for several seconds. Then he was aware of Annie standing beside him, her hand on his arm.

"You don't know what I did," he said. "It was all my fault."

"Tell me, then. How was it your fault?" Annie's voice was firmer, more full of determination.

He walked around the bench, and coming back, he sat again. Annie took her place beside him and waited. *Her patience must be stretched*, he thought. Summoning what courage he had, he decided to tell her everything.

"My sister, Lucy, was ill. Sheila told me not to go and see her, but I wanted to go. Her mum was round and driving me nuts. We had a bit of a row, so I stormed out and went home. I wanted a break."

"What was wrong with Lucy?"

"She had measles. There was no vaccination when I was born, so neither Lucy nor I had it as children, it turned out. Then as an adult, Lucy caught it — could have been from anywhere. I think I may have got it from her. I didn't have it badly at all. I wasn't even sure I did have it, to be honest. I had a cold. When I got home, Sheila told me not to go near the baby, so I didn't for about four days. If I hadn't gone to visit, it would have been okay. Our baby, Jo, was four months old. She wasn't even old enough to have had the vaccination. If we hadn't argued… I shouldn't have gone round to see Lucy. Sheila told me not to go. I'd just had enough of her mum always being there, and we were so tired and short of money. Jo must have caught measles from me. I must have brought it in on my clothes or something. I killed our baby."

Harry and Annie sat in silence for several seconds. Annie folded her arms.

It'll be any second now, Harry thought. *She'll get up and go, or maybe she'll shout at me first.*

"Harry, I'm not sure that's even possible."

"What?"

"To catch measles off clothing. Have you ever looked it up? I mean, you said you're not even sure you had it. She could have caught it from anywhere. It's spread via droplets when a person with the infection coughs or sneezes. If you didn't go near her for several days, it's highly unlikely you gave it to her."

Harry turned to look at her.

"Really, I mean it. It seems very unlikely it was from you. Harry, there are things I need to say to you, too."

Harry continued to sit hunched forward, his hands locked against contact.

"We've been friends, Harry, but when you kissed me, well... I knew it was more. It hit me like a rock. I shouldn't have been looking for something elsewhere when you were right in front of me. All that dating site stuff... Perhaps I needed to do that to see it. What I had with Rob was amazing, wonderful, and if he hadn't died, I'm sure it would be still. But he did die. I learned what it's like to lose someone. I'm not trying to invalidate your grief by telling you about mine. I'm saying I understand. There's been guilt, too, that he's gone and I'm still here. Now I understand, though: we owe it to those people who have passed on to live the best life we can. We shouldn't wallow in our self-pity and deny ourselves a life."

Harry turned his head and glimpsed her earnest expression. He felt a tear on his cheek and looked away with haste; then he felt the warmth of her hand on his arm again.

"It's taken me a while, but I've had to move on," Annie continued. "I've learned to cope on my own, and it's changed me. I'm more independent, which is why the dance school is so important to me. I need someone who understands that, now. Someone who is happy for me to follow my own thing but who's there to support me, too. I need *you*, Harry. What you have told me doesn't change any of that."

"You don't understand. It was my arrogant mistake that caused the loss of … of a *life*. I can't risk that again. I do love you, Annie. I have from the start. Probably since school, but you might want children. There's still time for that, and I…"

"Listen, Harry! I'm sure you can't catch measles from clothing. You're not even certain you came down with it?"

"No."

"Well, then … I don't believe you brought it back to your child. Let's look it up. I can't believe you haven't done that." Annie leaned forward and took both Harry's hands in hers, pulling them to her so he had to swivel and look at her. "It wasn't your fault, my darling Harry." She let go of his hands and put hers on either side of his face, wiping away the tears with her thumbs. Then she wrapped her arms around him. "I love you," she whispered. "I need you."

"Oh, Annie. I've wasted so many years, but then I may not have met you again when I did."

"I think the years between school and when we met again ensured we were ready for each other." Annie pulled back and he looked at her lovely face.

"Perhaps we complement each other," he said tentatively.

Annie's smile lit up her face and his spirit soared. "I think we do," she said and laughed through tears of her own.

"I want to kiss you again, Annie. May I?"

She laughed. "Do it."

Harry leaned towards her. His need was intense. Gently he took her face in his hands and his lips touched hers, warm and sensual. She put her arms around his waist and pulled him in. The kiss became joyous and deep and passionate. They stood, still locked together, so the length of their bodies touched. He was aware of all her curves.

"Can we go back to Lucy's?" Annie asked when she came up for air.

CHAPTER 30

Annie and Harry awoke within moments of each other as the sun was breaking through the early morning clouds. Annie looked across at him, his face close to hers on the pillow. She stretched luxuriously and smiled. Harry's arm came across her naked stomach before travelling further up.

"I hope Lucy didn't hear us last night," said Annie.

"I hope she doesn't hear us now," Harry replied, his dimple in evidence as he gave a cheeky grin. He leaned in to kiss her. Their lovemaking was generous and intense. They each had to touch and be touched. They both wanted to give, to heal, to show how each needed the other.

Some considerable time later, as they lay replete once again, Annie marvelled once more at this man beside her. "I can't believe how lucky I am," she said against his ear.

"I think I'm the fortunate one," Harry said. He gently took a strand of her hair and tucked it behind her ear. Then he became serious. "I know Rob was perfect for you, but I shall do everything in my power to ensure you're happy. I make this promise to you, Annie: I will cherish and support you. I'll love you forever, and never let you down." Harry's hand came up and he moved another wisp of hair from her forehead before he placed a feather-light kiss there.

"Rob was perfect at that stage in my life, Harry, but I've changed. I've had to. Now, I need other things. You, my love, are perfect for me now."

And he was. They had both been drifting, but now they had found each other. Gone was the awkwardness and insecurity of youth. They could each love with the confidence of experience, knowing what they needed and what they could do for the other.

As Annie left Mount's Bay behind, she knew she would always remember the view with great fondness. It was a place that had been good to her in her childhood, and now it held even stronger associations. Lucy had been so generous and next time Annie returned, as Harry's sister had urged, it would be with Harry.

They had to travel in their own cars. One stop for a quick lunch was all they had allowed themselves, because both were keen to return home. Annie had shared what had happened to the ballroom ceiling, and Harry wanted to ensure that the work could progress in good order. After all, Annie's livelihood was at stake, as well as his own.

At the end of their journey, as they followed each other past the disused gatehouse and along the driveway of Moondreams House, both saw that scaffolding encased the wing in question. Two men were on the roof. Annie felt like she had been away for weeks rather than days, and it was a relief to see the work taking place.

As she climbed out of the car, she stretched her bent limbs. Harry walked over, took her hand and led her towards the house, eager to see the damage to the ceiling.

They poked their heads through the door and surveyed it together. David joined them. The smell that Annie remembered was not as pungent, but it still hung in the air. Two more men were already working on the ceiling from the top of a tower of more scaffolding, while a third was pointing up from the floor and appeared to be directing operations.

"Heritage Roofing had a cancellation and were able to come and start work earlier than planned," David explained. "I've been getting a daily update from Tom, there. He doesn't say much, but he gives me the key information. You can see I've ensured they put down boards to protect the floor."

Annie privately marvelled at David's proactiveness and the energy in his demeanour. She would discuss it with Harry at the first opportunity. Could it be that this catastrophe, coupled with his interest in her dance school — and possibly Edith Hill — had reawakened his passion and snatched him from his depressive state?

"I think when all this is over and it's all restored, we should have a grand re-opening with a dance, don't you?" David turned to Annie. "Perhaps an evening ball where everyone can get dressed up — men in dinner jackets and ladies in gowns."

"That's a wonderful idea," Annie said.

"Yes, I could engage the Coronation Bar people. I was looking up their details. They are very experienced in running outside events. I say, Harry, what do you think?"

"That's a great thought. People would want to be able to have a drink."

"Yes, and catering. We'll have to think about that — nothing too complicated." David was on a roll now.

"I have a friend, and his daughter, Natalie, is a caterer. She doesn't normally do this kind of thing, I don't think, but she might consider it if it was easy finger buffet food. She started at my beginners' class recently. How long do you think this will all take?" Annie was thinking ahead, remembering that her students would be meeting in the entrance hall in a matter of days.

They discussed the work for a while longer before Annie reluctantly said she would have to return to collect her dog. She understood that Harry would have to tell David what had happened in the last forty-eight hours.

Before she slept that night, Annie received a text from Harry: *Goodnight, my darling. See you tomorrow. Xx*

She lay and soaked up his love and all that had happened between them.

Annie was drifting off to sleep when she had a sudden memory and bolted upright. Swinging her legs off the bed, she opened her underwear drawer. Fishing out a tiny wooden box that lay buried at the back, she returned to her bed. She hadn't seen this box for eighteen months or more. Her life had changed beyond all recognition since she'd placed it there.

The memories of that night returned, but they needed to be faced and put behind her. Opening the lid, she found the leaf. It was as dry and brown as it had been when she had pulled it from her hair on the night she'd lain beside her dead husband's grave, overcome with grief. She had been swamped with loneliness and longing for what should have been, but could never be.

As she looked at the dead leaf, tears welled. She tried to analyse her feelings. She was no longer wracked with sorrow, and she realised she was able to remember her marriage to Rob — and all she had experienced since — with gratitude. Only through those experiences would she have reached her present state. Tomorrow, she would return the leaf to the graveyard and draw a contented line beneath that era of her life.

EPILOGUE

Ellie and her friend Liv were set up at a table at the end of the path to collect tickets. They wore long dresses, which they'd previously used for a school prom, and David had bought them each a short, white, faux fur cape to keep them warm. At eighteen, they were exceedingly pleased with themselves, and were playing the ladies they were becoming with style and grace — mostly. Every so often, they would giggle over something the other observed.

The Coronation Bar people were set up in the entrance hall and had decorated the room with swags of white silk on a framework. Fresh arrangements of golden corn and barley, as well as artificial dark fruit and berries, disguised the frames. David had spared no expense in ensuring that everything complemented the new terracotta, white and pale blue décor in the ballroom. Groups of weighted helium balloons in shades of delicate blue and white shimmered and added a modern touch. The chandeliers had been professionally cleaned and the lights glittered. The curtains were still old, but the threadbare rug had been rolled and stored.

The ballroom itself had a new ceiling, and all the previous ornate plasterwork had been replicated. The floor had been protected well, and since the workmen had left it had been polished and made ready. White linen tablecloths covered the folding tables, and Annie had ensured each one had a centrepiece of the same grasses, fruit and berries as the bar. A huge arrangement also sat in the enormous fireplaces of each of the two rooms. The lights were dimmed to give a beautiful and intimate atmosphere.

Annie, Harry, and David stood at the door of the ballroom, waiting for dancers to arrive and greeting them as they did. The gasps and comments of appreciation continued as each couple entered the hall. This time, Annie had a space for coats and people were directed there before finding their tables. As soon as Edith Hill arrived, David excused himself to accompany her to her table, and there he chose to remain.

Annie's dress was new, and the green and brown shot fabric complemented her eyes and hair, and shimmered as she moved. The style emphasised her neat waist and curvy figure, and Harry had said, "You look stunning." Her skin was creamy smooth, with a residual tan from the long summer. Green drop earrings and a gold chain around her neck completed the whole. The emerald and diamonds on the third finger of her left hand caught the ambient light and shone for all to see.

They danced after she had put on the music. Fittingly, it was the first waltz they had shared at the previous dance. They swayed and glided to the music of 'The Sweetheart Tree'. Annie looked up at Harry and whispered, "My very own Harry Moon Dreams."

When Harry looked down at her, she could see his adoration in the glow of his eyes. Annie would tell him later of why *she* glowed so brightly. She would reassure him that all would be well with the child she was carrying.

A NOTE TO THE READER

Dear Reader,

When we returned to this country from living in France, my husband, much to my surprise and amazement, suggested we join a ballroom dancing class. There we made many friends with whom we are now close and we still enjoy this hobby.

On hearing I write books, as people are inclined to do, many fellow dancers suggested I write a book about our dance classes After several other novels, I have finally done just that although this story in no way reflects the truth of my experiences or the people I have met! It is pure fiction. However, I do recommend ballroom and Latin dancing as a means to fitness, fun, and friendship.

My thanks again go the team at Sapere Books for their cover design, editing, and marketing expertise. Without them, I as a writer, and you as a reader, would have missed much.

If you enjoyed reading *Rhythms of the Heart*, perhaps you might leave a brief review on **Amazon** or **Goodreads**. It doesn't need to be long; a couple of sentences will more than suffice. It will inform readers when choosing a book and would be a huge boost to this author. Thank you.

If you would like to know more about my writing, my website is **www.rosrendleauthor.co.uk**. Here you can also **sign up for my newsletter** where I often offer free gifts and timely access and information about forthcoming books. I'd love to hear from you, my dear reader, and you are able to chat with me via **Facebook** or via **Twitter.**

Thank you, again, and I hope we will meet again soon through the pages of one of my other books.

Ros Rendle

Sapere Books is an exciting new publisher of brilliant fiction and popular history.

To find out more about our latest releases and our monthly bargain books visit our website:
saperebooks.com